Finding Our Home

Longing for Home Book 3

Lisa Stanbridge

Crystal Brook Publishing

Trigger Warning: This novel contains references to brain tumours and related medical treatments, which may be triggering or upsetting for some readers.

This is a work of fiction. Names, characters and incidents portrayed are the product of the author's imagination. Any similarities to a name, character or history of any actual person, living or dead, is entirely coincidental.

FINDING OUR HOME

Copyright © 2023 by Lisa Stanbridge

The moral right of the author has been asserted

ISBN: 978-0-6456673-5-6

Also By Lisa Stanbridge

Longing for Home series:

Lonely in Paris – Book 1

Troubled in Paradise – Book 2

Finding Our Home – Book 3

Standalone books:

Abandoned Hearts

Navigate to the link below to read more about her books.

https://lisastanbridge.wixsite.com/lisastanbridgeauthor/books

For Tanya, Linda, Deb, and Kim.
Thanks for the Friday night chats and your constant support.

Chapter 1

Jane

Ever since I was little, I knew what I wanted in life. Meet Mr Right.

Get married.

Have children.

Building a career was sort of there in the background but it never took hold. If I enjoyed my job, I would be happy to turn it into one but that had never been the case...until recently.

Jacques asked again if I would work for Solutions Exécutives and I said yes. I'm so glad I did because I love going into the office together and working in the same environment. We don't step on each other's toes either because we both have very different roles.

If only he'd ask me another question I could say yes to...

Anyway, the fact is, life is falling into place. Slowly. But that's the issue.

Jacques tugs on my hand as he guides me through the patchy snow-covered streets of Paris, the streetlamps lighting our way. This winter hasn't been as cold as last year and there's been less snow. It snowed a few days before we arrived from the Gold Coast, but it's already melting. It's mid-January, so the weather is beginning to turn as spring approaches.

I crunch on a twig and glance across at Jacques with what I'm sure is a sappy smile. Oh, how I adore this man. Just over two years we've been together, and yeah things may be moving slower than I'd like, but it doesn't change how I feel about him.

"Where are we going?" I ask as we round a corner.

He glances at me with a boyish grin, his eyes shining as we pass a lamp. "It's a surprise."

"A surprise?" I gasp and stop. "Oh. My. Goodness."

"What's wrong?" He turns to me, brow furrowed.

I wrap my arms around his neck and hug him, laughing and jumping in excitement. "I can't believe it!"

"Jane." He pulls back and studies my face. "What's going on?"

"You just used a contraction," I say, bouncing on the balls of my feet. "Actually, it was *three*."

Yes, this is a small thing, but the whole time I've known him, he's never *ever* used them. He always speaks precisely with full words. It's what I love about him, but this is so unexpected.

"What?" Jacques drops my arms and steps back, shaking his head. "I do not understand."

Now he's back to normal. I grin at him and loop my arm through his as we start walking. "A contraction," I explain, "is when you combine two words to make one. You know, 'it is' becomes 'it's' or 'will not' becomes 'won't' or 'do not' becomes 'don't.'"

He glances across at me in horror. "Is that what they are called?" He holds the back of his free hand against his forehead, and dramatically says, "*Oh la la* I have been in Australia too long."

The horror is replaced by a grin and I giggle, squeezing his arm as we keep walking. I'm giddy from this turn of events.

We continue our stroll in silence. We have both been so busy and tonight we finally have some time together. After dinner, Jacques suggested an evening walk. No way could I refuse! One of my favourite things is exploring the streets of Paris. It's even better if it's at night. The sky is clear, dotted with faint stars, difficult to make out through the light pollution. The crescent moon pops in and out of view between the tall buildings.

Jacques has a set destination, and I am content to follow.

My phone beeps and I remove it from my jacket pocket. It's a text from Mum. A quick calculation in my head tells me it's four thirty a.m. in Adelaide. Goodness, she's up early.

"Wednesday?" I screech, coming to a sudden halt.

Jacques stumbles to a stop beside me. "What is it?"

I show him the message.

Good morning Jane, change of plans! Your father and I are off to the airport. First stop London for a few days then Paris! I'll send you the itinerary. We'll be there on Wednesday. I hope this isn't inconvenient.

I blink a couple of times as everything pieces together in my head. I *should* be surprised, but I'm not. Ever since Mum's successful surgery and treatment for her brain tumour, she's now living life to the fullest. Remission, it seems, has this effect on people.

We text each other good morning or good night every day, and other little messages when something interesting happens. After the doctor cleared her for travel, nothing stops her. She and Dad go away often or have nights out. They'd planned to visit Paris in a few months' time. And *that's* the surprise.

Wednesday?

"This is very last minute," I explain to Jacques. "We're flying home next week."

He shrugs and wraps his arm around my shoulders, guiding me along as we start walking again. "We can reschedule, can we not?"

"Of course, but I don't understand the suddenness."

"Was it not you who encouraged me to live in the moment?"

He grins at me and I chuckle. "Okay, fair point. Can I leave you to deal with our flights once I receive Mum and Dad's travel details? I'll organise an itinerary of things to do while they're here."

He nods and we continue in silence. I type back a quick reply and pocket my phone. I *am* excited to see them again and show them around.

Jacques and I went back to Adelaide for Mum's surgery, then returned to Surfers Paradise. They've been so busy since, we now only see them on our weekly video chats. We only recently returned to Paris to finalise legal matters over Marcel's will.

There was a hold up with the probate, but it's sorted now. On Monday Jacques will be meeting with his family, including Avril. The reading of a will is not a requirement here to process the probate, so apart from Angélique, no one else in the DuPont family knows about Avril's existence. Oh, to be a fly on the wall.

Once that's finalised, the only thing missing will be the rest of my life goal. I have my Mr Right. Now I want marriage and children. I'm *so* ready.

We enter through double iron gates into a park lit up with lamps evenly spaced along a pathway that goes through the middle. We pass other people also enjoying an evening walk and we all share smiles in greeting.

I now only need the answer to one question: Is Jacques as ready as I am?

I gaze at him as he stops and scratches his head through his hat. He appears confused as he turns one way then another. Taking out his phone, he checks something, nods, and leads me away. I follow dutifully, my mind drifting back to my life goals.

Let's be honest here. These were set in place from a young age while still playing with dolls. As I married them off to make believe partners, I dreamt of my future. My naïve self expected to meet Mr. Right by the time I turned twenty and marry a couple of years later.

These ages were so set in my head, it should be no surprise that when I was fifteen-and-a-half and experienced my first *real* crush, I was a teeny bit obsessive. With less than five years to find Mr. Right, time was ticking.

The problem? He didn't share my feelings.

I went through an embarrassingly awkward time, sending him love notes in class, even stalking him at school. On my sixteenth birthday I wanted to experience my first kiss with him. Even told him so to his face, but he said no. My young, hormonal, and naïve self didn't take 'no' for an answer.

What ensued was an embarrassing chase through the streets. *Me* chasing *him*, that is, while begging for a kiss. In the end he outran me, leaving me crying in shame and embarrassment. My parents grounded me for stalking—how many teenagers can say they were grounded for that? —and I learnt a hard lesson in consent and that it applies to everyone.

In better news, I *did* have my sweet sixteen kiss. It may not have been on my birthday, but the boy at least liked me back.

Fast forward another sixteen years and I like to think I've matured and become a semi-reasonable adult. I dismissed my unrealistic goals and let life take me on a journey.

That's why I'm now nearly thirty-three years old and still not married.

And there is the problem. Now it's getting silly.

I *do not* want to ever be that teenage version of myself again. I won't scare poor Jacques into a proposal, but *geez*, can he please hurry up?

I shake the worries out of my head. I'm doing better at not over-worrying about things, I'm not about to start now.

We pass a couple of benches, one on either side of the path, and in front of us is a beautiful three-tier cast stone fountain. There is no water trickling from it, but the large basin on the ground is full. In the distance is the city in all its glory, the moon centred between two buildings. To the left is the stunning Eiffel Tower.

"Wow," I breathe, spinning around to face Jacques. As I do so, my foot slips on an unmelted patch of ice. Everything goes in slow motion.

The same moment I slip, I notice him on bended knee, holding open a small, square, velvet box. My heart leaps and I wonder if he's a mind reader, but then I become horrifyingly aware that I've lost my balance and I'm falling forward. My arms flail, but I can't stop my fall.

Time speeds up as Jacques jumps to his feet to help, but my hand knocks the box out of his hand. He steadies me, then we lunge forward in a desperate attempt to grab the box and the ring hurtling towards the fountain. We clumsily fall against each other and land on the snow-covered ground in a jumble of arms and legs, hearing a *plop* as it falls into the water.

Jacques stares at me, eyes shining with humour, cheeks flushed in the artificial light. I stare back, startled, and we burst out laughing. People walk past smiling but have no clue what's going on.

I *can't* believe I ruined the moment I was wishing would happen for decades.

"I'm so sorry." I gasp for air only to start laughing again.

Jacques shakes his head and stands, going over to the fountain to peer into the basin. He takes a deep breath before he removes his coat and pushes the sleeve of his shirt up to his elbow. He sticks his arm into the water with a gasp.

"*Merde* it is freezing," he says, his breath catching.

He pulls his arm out quickly, box *and* ring still intact. I sigh with relief and get to my feet, my laughter fading as Jacques comes back over, his face serious but humour dancing in his eyes.

"With you nothing is normal." He smiles. "And that is the way I always want it." He falls to his knee once more. People passing by stop to watch. "I love you just the way you are, Jane Collins. Will you do me the honour of being my wife?"

Tears trickle down my cheeks and I hold my hands to my mouth. Unable to find words, I nod but it appears to be enough. Grinning, Jacques gets to his feet and takes off my lefthand glove. He removes the promise ring and I take it from him, putting it in my jeans pocket.

In its place he slips on the cold, wet engagement ring. Even though I've seen it before, it still takes my breath away. It's so perfect sitting on my finger. The teardrop diamond shimmers back at me on its simple gold band.

"Is this actually happening?" I whisper, glancing at him through tear-filled eyes.

"Yes, it's really happening."

I swallow the lump in my throat and gaze at the ring once more. This is what I wanted. What I *want*. But planning a wedding when I've got to think about Jacques' family? Oh boy...

Chapter 2

Jacques

Sunday night Jane and I celebrate by going back to where it all began.

Francette.

This time we are not only joined by my best friend Claude and his wife Penny, but also my brother Rémy, and the Kilpatricks—Aimée, Tavish, and Avril. Aimée was my au pair when I was a child and we lost contact for many years. We made contact again last year and she is like a mother to me. Tavish is her husband and Avril is her daughter...and my half-sister.

Jane and I have not announced our engagement yet, waiting for the right moment.

The waitress returns with our drinks, then leaves after taking our food order. As if on cue, the La Tour Eiffel starts sparkling and a glance at my watch tells me it is seven p.m. Now is as good a time as ever. I nudge Jane's shoulder and when she glances at me, I raise my eyebrows in silent question. She smiles and nods.

Before gaining everyone's attention, I glance around at the group of family and friends. Rémy and I have a better relationship now and he is the only member of my family I have frequent contact with. I am still not sure if I will tell Maman or Céleste about the engagement. I have had little contact with them over the last few months. Only a handful of necessary conversations in the early days of submitting documents for the probate. It is telling that many months have passed and we have had nothing to do with each other.

If the topic comes up tomorrow, I suppose I will mention it. But I have no intention of inviting them to the wedding.

My only concern about tomorrow is how my family will react when they meet Avril. Or, more specifically, when *she* announces herself. In all her naivety, Avril is excited about being able to waltz in and announce who she is. I love her, but even though I have warned her about my family and what they are capable of, she does not take me seriously. Yes, she is a grown adult and can take care of herself, but I am still worried.

I only hope my worries will come to nothing.

Céleste may be more accepting. She settled into a receptionist role at Entreprises DuPont after Papa's will stated she must have a job. Rémy manages her and reports back to me regularly that she is doing well. Considering she has never worked a day in her life this surprises me, but it gives me hope that she may accept Avril's appearance.

There's a kick to my shin under the table and I wince, turning to Jane who's frowning at me. I smile in apology and shake myself back to the present. I should not be thinking about tomorrow. Tonight is for celebrating.

I clear my throat to gain everyone's attention, open my mouth to speak, but Jane loses patience and jumps to her feet. "We're engaged!" she squeals, holding out her hand.

There is silence for a nanosecond, followed by a round of cheers. Avril is the first to jump up and run around, embracing Jane then me.

I cannot even be annoyed that Jane stole the announcement. I am happy that she is so excited. She gazes at me briefly with an apologetic smile before basking in the excitement. There are congratulations all around then the questions start.

When is the wedding?

Where will the wedding be?

Who will be in the wedding party?

They keep on coming and we are shocked into silence until I find my voice. "We have only just got engaged," I say with a laugh. "We have not discussed any of those details yet."

Our food arrives and I am relieved that everyone is too focused on eating to ask more questions. I glance over at Jane who is digging into her pasta, a smile fixed to her face. She turns to me. "I think we should have a beach wedding," she whispers.

"In Surfers Paradise?"

"Not necessarily. Maybe we could consider a halfway mark. Somewhere like The Maldives."

"Are you sure? You do not wish to marry in Australia?"

She shrugs one shoulder. "I would love to, but it's unfair to make people on one side of the world travel further than the other. Besides," she sends me a cheeky smile, "if we want to go on a European honeymoon, we won't have so far to fly back."

I chuckle and wrap my arm around her shoulders. "European honeymoon? You have it all figured out, don't you?"

She nods, her eyes sparkling. "I love it when you use contractions." She leans up to peck my lips. "What do you think though?"

"About contractions?" I frown, baffled with why she is so hung up on this. I may not have always used them, but it is more natural now.

"No," she laughs with a shake of her head, "about my wedding and honeymoon suggestions."

"Oh, I think they are wonderful ideas. I have never been to The Maldives. Or anywhere for that matter, apart from Australia."

She pokes me in the ribs. "I know, what's with that? Why hadn't you travelled before meeting me, despite having so much money?"

I shrug and sip my champagne. "I love my city so I was never inclined to. Besides, I had no one to enjoy it with." I stare into her eyes when I add, "With you though, I would go anywhere."

We share a smile then Jane turns to Penny and starts talking. I don't think she will ever fully know how much she has changed my life.

❧❧❧

Monday comes around and it is a mad rush to make it to work on time. We are both working from the Paris office while we are here. Not only did we oversleep after a late night at Francette, but Jane lured me back to bed this morning.

We smile at each other as the elevator travels up the floors to our level and I squeeze Jane's hand. I like mornings like these, but they do not happen often. They happened more in Surfers Paradise. Life speeds by at a faster pace in Paris. I am surprised by how much I miss life in Queensland. Paris will always be in my heart, but Australia is home now.

The elevator reaches our level. We step out and kiss each other goodbye. Jane goes one way while I go the other. Her job covers Australia and Paris, but as we continue to grow so does her workload. Soon she will need to hire someone to assist her. Preferably someone here so when we return to Australia, she will only have to focus on one country.

I greet a good morning to the receptionist and wave to Claude in his office before entering mine, surprised to find Rémy seated at my desk.

"What are you doing here?" I ask, placing my satchel in my drawer.

"Good morning to you too," he quips.

I sit down and open my laptop, powering it on. "Sorry, I did not expect you today. We didn't have a meeting, did we?"

A flash of unreadable emotion passes across his face. "No, but I need to talk to you. I can wait if you are busy. I do not have meetings until this afternoon."

I enter the password on my computer. "No, I am free until ten. You couldn't have told me last night?"

"I did not want to bother your celebration with work talk." He opens his mouth to say something else but ends up saying nothing.

"What?" I ask, sitting back in my chair.

He shrugs. "There is something different about you."

I flash him a grin. "I'm engaged now."

"No, it is not that." He shakes his head. "Never mind, you are probably just lovesick or something." He smirks. "I am happy for you and Jane, she is a great woman." He wears a wistful expression as he gazes out the window.

"She is, but you are not here about that, correct?"

He turns back, avoiding eye contact. "Correct. There is something I need to tell you, Jacques." He looks up and meets my gaze. "About Entreprises DuPont."

I study him through narrowed eyes. I may have no interest in the company, but I have tried to keep on top of everything. It is what a good CEO would do, although it is usually through Rémy's updates. I do not always see the data, so in that area, I have fallen short.

"What is it?" I ask.

Rémy puffs out a breath. "I want to resign."

Chapter 3

Jane

An invitation lands in my inbox from Jacques. It's for us to have a meeting tomorrow with a journalist to discuss an official engagement announcement in the *Nouvelles Quotidiennes de Paris*, or Paris Daily News.

I squirm in my seat. While I don't deal with a lot of media attention, this is enough to make me uncomfortable. This never happens in Queensland, only here. It makes sense, but the Plain Jane's of the world are not built for it. I guess that's what comes with dating the 'Rogue DuPont'.

Yep, a random local magazine dubbed him that once...*once*...and it stuck. I find it quite funny, but Jacques hates it. He might've lightened up over the last couple of years, but he'll always have his serious side. Especially when it comes to business.

At least the journalist is one we trust. The same one Claude set Jacques up with last year when he made a statement about his time in Australia. Jacques usually has control over the media hype, so it rarely gets out of hand, but it doesn't make being in the spotlight any easier. I'm doing my best at being the dutiful girlfriend...no, wait, *fiancée*...and standing beside him, while still keeping tabs on who I am. I'm just thankful he doesn't seek attention. He does what's necessary for both companies, but that's it.

I accept the invite then return to work. My phone buzzes a few minutes later. Picking it up, I grin when I spot a message from Bella. The vet in Australia. She's not just our local vet anymore, we've become great friends. She always takes care of Moe when we're in Paris. Our not-so-little adult cat.

I swipe the screen and a photo appears of him sitting regally on a chair with a little beret on his head, followed by a text.

Found this today, isn't he just *so* French?

I chuckle and type back a reply.

I love it! Is he okay?

We text back and forth for a couple of minutes, talking about Moe, who's doing well much to my relief, and discussing the change in plans about our return. Not that I know any dates yet, but I can at least warn her.

As our conversation is coming to an end, I send one more text.

Would you like to be one of my bridesmaids?

I reread it with a cringe. One of? Far out, how many am I even thinking of? Since the proposal, I've had nothing but wedding ideas floating through my mind. Despite knowing what I wanted in life, I never gave the actual wedding a thought. When I played pretend weddings as a kid, they were always white and extravagant, nothing more.

Now, I've got so much to think about. Who to invite, who *not* to invite. Where we'll marry. We might've agreed on finding somewhere halfway, but that's it. The Maldives was only a suggestion. I should research other options too. But before that, we need to set a date and estimate guest numbers.

Ugh.

Okay, stop. Take a breath. Start again.

First step: buy a wedding planner book.

I suppose I could hire a professional planner. Jacques wouldn't care, he's always saying 'my money is your money' which I appreciate but if I'm keeping myself grounded, I won't splash out *that* much. I want to set a budget and stick to it. Plus, I quite like the idea of planning a wedding.

My phone buzzes again, a reply from Bella. Loads of excited emojis and 'YES' written about ten times. She sends another one telling me she's going to bed since she's starting early.

After sending her a goodnight text, I think about who the 'others' will be. Avril for the other bridesmaid, and Penny as my Matron of Honour. I send them messages and receive instant 'yes' replies from both. Well, that's one thing ticked off the list I suppose.

Grinning, I put my phone away and return to work. The morning is a blur of emails, tech support tickets, and meetings. At midday I make my way to Jacques' office so we can grab some lunch. Since he's going out for the will meeting at one p.m. I'm taking my break earlier.

When I reach it, I knock on the doorframe and walk in. He lifts his head and throws me a weak smile. He must've had a rough morning.

"You want to eat now before you go to the reading?"

He rakes a hand through his hair. "Yes, I could do with a break."

After donning our coats and scarves, we make our way downstairs to Le Petit Café Parisien down the road. Jacques appears deep in thought, but I don't disturb him. There's a crease in his brow like something is bothering him.

I grab a seat while he places the order. When he returns to the table, he has his phone in his hand and he's typing.

When our coffee and sandwiches arrive, Jacques doesn't notice at first. He's scrolling now, so I pluck it out of his hand. He glances at me in surprise as I place it face down.

"Lunch time, you can deal with work stuff later."

He smiles in apology. "Sorry, it's been a tough morning."

"What happened?"

He sips his drink. "Rémy wants to resign."

"He *what*?" I drop the serviette I'm unfolding.

He picks up his sandwich, sighs, and puts it back on the plate again. "He said he doesn't want to be in business anymore." He grinds his jaw then takes a sip of his coffee. "After all I did for him. Trained him, mentored him, and helped him become the businessman he is today. And for what? He's just going to throw it away?"

I place the serviette in my lap because I *always* make a mess. The sandwiches here are amazing, full of filling but super messy.

"What does he want to do?" I pick up my sandwich and bite into it.

"That's just it." He puts his cup back on the saucer too hard, causing the liquid to slop over the edge. "He doesn't know."

He mutters under his breath as he lifts the top off his sandwich and removes the red onion. He'll eat it in anything, just not raw.

"You could have ordered it without onion," I say.

"I forgot to ask," he mumbles, putting the bread back on and taking a bite, chewing slowly. His brow is creased and a frown tugs on his lips.

"Hey." I reach out and place my hand on his. "Not everyone is as great as you."

He raises his eyebrows and tries to smile but it's more of a grimace. "That is not what I'm implying."

I chuckle and move my hand back. "I know, but it made you smile, didn't it?"

He smiles a little easier this time.

"But seriously," I continue, "what I *am* saying is not everyone is going to be a natural like you. Rémy isn't. You've trained him to do well, but if he doesn't enjoy it, why should he have to keep doing it?"

His shoulders slacken and he chuckles. "How do you always know the right thing to say?"

I shrug and sip my coffee. "It's not what you want to hear though."

He shakes his head. "Maybe not, but you're still right."

I shudder and sigh. "I love it when you use contractions *and* tell me I'm right. It's such a turn on."

His cheeks turn a bright red and I grin at him. We laugh and he grabs his serviette, gently whacking my arm with it.

"What are you going to do?" I ask a few minutes later once Jacques has devoured his sandwich and I'm halfway through mine. "Advertise for someone else?"

"No, I spoke to Rémy and he's on board with this. I'm going to merge Entreprises DuPont with Solutions Exécutives."

I gasp, choking on a crumb. I cough and cough, reaching for my coffee and taking a slurp, eyes watering.

"Are you serious?" I wheeze. "Is that possible under the conditions of the will?"

He nods and fills me in. He's got it all planned and while it sounds daunting, I'll have very little to do with it in the beginning. Once the merger is complete, however long that takes, I'll have a team to manage.

"Wow." I wipe my mouth with a serviette and set my empty plate on top of Jacques'. "You've got it all figured out. What will your mum say? I thought she still had some hold over it through a clause in the will?"

His eyes darken and he sits up straight. "The stipulation was that I could not *sell* the company while she was alive. Since she has no actual position, and she holds no shares, she will be notified of the merger but have no say in it."

I nod and finish off my coffee. The air always grows tense when I mention Angélique or his late father, so I change the topic.

"So, I've got my bridesmaids sorted."

Jacques relaxes in his seat but eyes me curiously. "Brides*maids*, as in more than one?"

"Um, yes?" I bite my bottom lip when it occurs to me that we've never discussed weddings and different traditions. "In Australia we have an equal number of bridesmaids to groomsmen."

"Interesting." He thinks for a moment. "Most French weddings I have been to do not have either, they have two witnesses instead."

"Oh." Have I been too hasty? "Well—"

"But I do not mind doing it your way," Jacques adds. "I am not hung up on tradition."

I breathe a little easier. "Okay, if you're sure. I've chosen Penny as my Matron of Honour, and Bella and Avril are my bridesmaids."

His eyes widen. "Three? Do I even know three men I can have as groomsmen?"

"You know lots of people."

He stares at me deadpan. "Not all of them are people I want standing next to me at my wedding."

"Fair enough, but I'm sure Claude will be one, right?" He nods, and I continue, "If you can only have one, we don't have to completely follow the Australian tradition."

"This coming from a 'shameless traditionalist'?" he uses his fingers as quotations.

"Well." I run my finger along the handle of my mug. "I don't have to follow all the traditions I suppose. What about Rémy?"

He pauses in contemplation. "I will think about it." He checks the time. "I should go. It is nearly one o'clock."

On the way out, I say, "I want to start looking at locations. Any suggestions on dates?"

We step out onto the cobblestone pathway and stand to the side of the door. Jacques glances one way then the other before settling on me. "I have not thought about it." He reaches out to cup my cheek, stroking it. "There is no urgency, is there?"

"No, of course not." I cover his hand with mine, feeling bad for bringing it up when he's got a lot on his plate. "We can talk about it later. I hope everything goes well."

He raises his eyes heavenward and mutters, "*Ooh la la,*" under his breath, then louder he adds, "the sooner it is over, the better. I will see you back at the office."

He leans in and kisses me before rushing off for the reading. I stare after him, gnawing my bottom lip. This is the DuPont family we're talking about. There will be some kind of drama, there always is.

Chapter 4

Jacques

My stomach tightens into a knot as I approach the lawyer's office. I am looking forward to this being over. What will become of us after today? Maman, I have no idea, nor do I care. As for myself, Rémy, and Céleste, we will have complete control of our lives at long last.

Rémy is already planning a life without Entreprises DuPont and our controlling family. His resignation is proof of that. I still have not come to terms with it, but I respect his decision. Jane is right, he should not have to stay in a job he dislikes.

Céleste, I do not know what she will do. I always thought she and Maman would live together in misery, but reconnecting with Rémy has opened my eyes. Learning that Céleste has changed after working for Entreprises DuPont, is it possible that she is not as bad as I once thought? Maybe she too only needs a chance, like Rémy. I am intrigued to see what conversations we have today. If any.

I feel guilty for not giving her a chance before now. I could not move past the moment she said she wanted nothing to do with me. While this was true once upon a time, it might not be anymore. If

I have changed over the years, as has Rémy, there is every likelihood Céleste has too.

Perhaps today we will have the opportunity to reconnect as siblings, Avril included.

As if on cue, Avril turns a corner and we approach the office from different directions. When she spots me, she grins and waves wildly before breaking into a run and flinging herself at me when we meet. She laughs gleefully as though we have not seen each other for months. It has only been a few hours.

It is frightening how much I care for my baby sister. All I want to do is protect her. She may be an adult, but she is still so young and naïve. But I must not smother her.

"I'm so excited!" she exclaims as she steps back.

My heart thumps. "Excited?"

She visibly reins in her emotions and smiles. "Sorry, it sounds awful but it's not every day I inherit money."

Fair call. I may not understand what is so exciting about it, but I am also aware her life is different from mine. Aimée and Tavish have provided the essentials, but it has never been easy financially. After they contracted my company last year to help their business improve, it is doing well. They have worked hard to get where they, and their contract will be ending soon.

Once the inheritance has been divided, Avril has big plans to start her own interior design business here in Paris. Her excitement is justified. This is life-changing for her.

I glance at the time on my wrist. Five minutes until the appointment time.

"I should go inside," I say. "I am sure the rest of my family will be here already. I suggest you make an appearance in about ten minutes."

Avril notes the time and nods, beaming at me. Her once dyed red hair is now dark brown, her natural colour. It makes her appear more like Aimée, but the DuPont genes are coming through in her eyes and nose.

Pushing open the door, I step into the warm office. I unwrap my scarf from around my neck and pull off my gloves. The door clicks shut after me and I stand in front of the empty reception desk.

Maybe I *am* taking this whole thing too seriously. Perhaps it is time to go along with it. After all, this is the final step in removing Papa from our lives. Besides, there is no stopping the little thrill of knowing I will inherit more money. I cannot change what has been hardwired into me. Once a DuPont, always a DuPont I suppose.

At least now I feel more in control. Jane helped me in so many ways and we do not bicker over it the way we used to.

The receptionist appears from the back room. She recognises me and directs me to an office on the left. When I enter, the lawyer is sitting at a large oak desk with Maman, Céleste, and Rémy opposite him.

"Monsieur Laurent," I greet the lawyer.

He nods in greeting and gestures for me to take a seat next to Rémy. As I do so, I glance across at my family. Rémy nudges my shoulder and smiles. Céleste, much to my surprise, sends me a smile too. Maman does not look at me. Her back is ramrod straight, head held high, hands folded in her lap, face devoid of emotion.

"Shall we proceed?" Monsieur Laurent says in French when it ticks over to one p.m.

"Why must we all be here?" Céleste whines. "We are already aware of who's getting what." She folds her slim arms.

"Do not start," Maman hisses. "Please continue, Monsieur."

Céleste huffs but says nothing more. When no one else speaks, Monsieur Laurent continues, "We are here today to read the last will and testament of Monsieur Marcel DuPont and divide the assets according to his will." He glances at Céleste. "This is the final step, Madame. I will require some information and signatures from all of you."

Monsieur Laurent places his glasses on the end of his nose and opens the leather folder on his desk. After clearing his throat, he picks up the will and starts reading. "The DuPont estate and all its assets will be left to Madame Angélique DuPont, along with the DuPont fortune."

I glance across at Maman, curious at her reaction, but of course she remains as stoic as ever.

"The company of Entreprises DuPont, all its assets, and financials will be left to Monsieur Jacques DuPont, who is to be the sole owner but may choose the ongoing staff at his own discretion. Apart from Monsieur Rémy DuPont and Madame Céleste DuPont who must have positions within the company. It cannot be sold at any point while Madame Angélique DuPont is alive."

This time a smug smile flickers to life on Maman's face.

Monsieur Laurent continues, "There is also one other clause here that may be of interest to you, Jacques." He pushes his glasses up his nose. "It states that you have complete control over any future partnerships, the only prohibition is the sale of the company." He glances up at me with raised eyebrows. "Is that clear?"

I nod. Even though I have known this for a while, it is a relief to have it confirmed. It is the key to merging the company with mine. I will most likely enlist Monsieur Laurent's help with the legalities of the merger.

Rémy nudges my shoulder, and we share a smile. Maman will find out later, we will not reveal our plans just yet.

Monsieur Laurent continues reading other clauses that do not affect me when there is a commotion outside. It must be Avril.

Merde. I did not consider the prospect of the receptionist stopping her entrance. I am about to sort it out when the door bursts open and she stumbles in, grabbing my chair. She looks down at me, her face red, and mouths 'sorry'.

She freezes and takes in the room and the bewildered faces of my family.

"Uh," is all she manages, her eyes widening.

"Who are you?" Monsieur Laurent demands in French, placing the will on the leather folder.

Avril glances from him to me, looking panicked. "I'm sorry, I don't understand French."

Monsieur Laurent sighs but before he speaks, I stand and slide my arm across her shoulders. The poor girl is shaking. Now I feel terrible for agreeing to let her do this. I should have pre-empted that when the time came it would be overwhelming for her.

It is too late now.

"I apologise, Monsieur," I say in English. "I would like to introduce Avril Kilpatrick, she is—"

"It's okay," Avril whispers. "I've got this now."

"Are you sure?"

She nods and smiles weakly. "I owe Ma this much." She stands tall and confident. I sit back down. "My mother—"

"Wait," I interrupt in a whisper, "we agreed to keep her out of this."

She places a gentle hand on my shoulder and squeezes. "Trust me, I spoke to Ma about this. It's okay." She clears her throat, and continues, "My mother is Aimée Kilpatrick, nee Dubois. She worked as an au pair for the DuPont family for four years. During her last year in this position, Monsieur Marcel DuPont forced himself upon her—"

A gasp cuts through the tension and I glance across at Céleste who is holding a hand to her mouth. I peer at Maman who is staring straight ahead, still stoic and emotionless. I am still under the impression she knew about it, but not certain. Rémy is staring at me with questions in his eyes. I have a lot of explaining to do, but I hope he will forgive me for keeping this secret.

"—which resulted in me," Avril continues, pointing to herself. "The DuPonts, that is Marcel and Angélique, paid her for her silence and forced her to sign a non-disclosure agreement." She fumbles in her bag and retracts a folded envelope, handing it to the lawyer. "Whether intended or not, the NDA has an end date, which has now passed."

My breath catches. An end date? This is unexpected and explains why Aimée was willing to reveal her identity. Not only did Papa make an 'all natural children' clause in his will, but he overlooked the date on the non-disclosure. This cannot be intentional. He would want to keep it secret for as long as possible.

Papa always gave the impression he knew what he was doing and never made mistakes. There is a strange sense of relief knowing he made a lot of them. They are now allowing justice to be served.

"As the legitimate child of Marcel DuPont," Avril continues, "I should also be here." She releases a shaky breath and I throw her an encouraging smile.

I am so proud. She puts a hand on my shoulder, and I place mine over it.

Monsieur Laurent reads over the documents, tsking and shaking his head.

"What are they?" I whisper to Avril.

She crouches beside me. "The original NDA, my birth certificate, and DNA results that confirms I'm your sister."

I frown. "When did this all come about?"

"Ma told me they forced her to have the test while I was still in the womb, which led her to being paid out and forced to sign the document."

My heart goes out to Aimée. She did not tell me this, but I do not blame her. It must be painful to talk about.

"Well, well, well," Monsieur Laurent switches to English, placing the papers down, "we do have another DuPont to consider in the will. I must take copies of these, is that acceptable, Madame Kilpatrick?"

Avril nods and stands again.

"Do you want my chair?" I ask.

"I will bring in another," Monsieur Laurent says before Avril can respond.

"Were you aware of this?" Rémy asks.

"What is going on?" Céleste asks.

Their questions keep coming in rapid fire but we cannot answer them as Monsieur Laurent returns with a chair and the room falls silent. I will answer them later. Avril sits and all eyes turn to Maman who is sitting in her normal regal position, lips pursed, face expressionless. How does she do it?

"Wait a minute," Céleste says, getting to her feet and turning to Maman, "*you* knew about this? You kept this from us?" She pales and sways on her feet.

I jump up. "Are you okay?"

"*And* you!" She steadies herself and spins around to face me, her fierce gaze betraying her anger and hurt. "You knew this intruder existed and said nothing!"

"I only found out recently." I do not think saying 'months' will help the situation. "I knew nothing about what Papa did before that."

She lets out a high-pitched squeal, which makes my ears ring. "I am so *done* with this family! Monsieur Laurent, will you please hurry up and finish this so I can leave? I want nothing to do with these people ever again."

I glance at Rémy then at Céleste, both looking hurt and confused.

When Monsieur Laurent goes to speak, I say, "Apologies Monsieur. Céleste, Rémy, can we talk first? Maman does not need to be included, but as siblings we should get together."

Céleste opens her mouth then closes it, glares at Avril and says, "Fine, but *she* is not invited." She points to Avril.

"Yes, she is, because she is the innocent party here, as are the rest of us. Whether we like it or not, Marcel DuPont is a father to all of us, but do we want him to keep us separated forever?"

Rémy, to my surprise, shakes his head and Céleste does too after a moment.

"How about we go somewhere after we are done here?" I suggest. "Can we all take the afternoon off?" My siblings nod. "It is settled. Please proceed Monsieur Laurent."

The poor lawyer shakes his head and continues with no further interruptions. When the meeting ends, we all provide the required identification, sign the paperwork, then Maman leaves without a word to anyone.

Chapter 5

Jane

I'm not surprised that Jacques doesn't return to the office. When he messages me around two p.m. saying he and his siblings are going to locate a bar, I get the impression it's been a stressful occasion.

My biggest surprise is when he mentions they're *all* going. Including Céleste.

Interesting.

When the clock ticks over to five p.m., I stay a little later to finish off some work, bidding everyone goodnight as they filter out the door. My phone pings with a message from Jacques.

We are still at Le Salon du Clair de Lune. You are welcome to join us.

I bite my lip as I consider this. Drinks after work occasionally occur on a Friday but never on a Monday. Today *is* an exception though. My only hesitation is Céleste since I've never officially met her. Might as well get it over with now, right? According to Rémy and Jacques, she's making an effort, so I should too.

Sure, I'll be there in about half an hour.

When Marcel died, an obvious divide formed with Jacques and Rémy on one side, Angélique and Céleste on the other. Avril's surprise appearance will change a lot of things.

Fifteen minutes later, I shut down my computer and stand, placing the strap of my handbag over my shoulder. On the way to the door, I switch off the lights in my area. I'm about to check the rest of the office when Claude appears, flicking off the light switches at his end of the building. I head to the door and hold it open.

"I didn't realise you were still here," I say.

He flicks the final switch and steps past me into the hallway. "Just finishing up a few things."

I lock up and we go to the elevators. Once on the street, we start walking in the same direction. I wrap my scarf around my neck and don my gloves, shivering as the chilly breeze bites at my cheeks.

"It's like the old days, isn't it?" Claude glances at me sideways. "You and me working together again."

"Yeah but at least you're not my boss this time."

"Well, technically I am. But so is your fiancé."

I gasp in surprise. "No—" But then I think about it. Business partners. Duh. "Oh crap, you're right."

Claude laughs as we cross a road.

"Listen, I have a favour to ask," he says when we're back on the path, sidestepping a pedestrian walking too close. "Penny's been a bit off." He pauses for a moment. "She could do with a friend."

I stop and step to the side. Claude stops too, standing in front of me. His cheeks are flushed but he won't make eye contact.

"Is everything okay?" Every possible worst-case scenario tries to enter my mind but I push them away. "It's nothing terrible, is it?"

He meets my gaze. "No, nothing like that. It's just something I think she needs to tell you. So, you'll talk to her?"

"Yeah of course, I'll text her. I want to go dress shopping for the wedding soon, that should perk her up."

He smiles in relief. "Thanks, Jane."

We start walking again, chatting about Amélie and Henri and life in general.

After two blocks, Claude says, "This is my turn, catch you tomorrow."

We wave at each other. He goes to the left while I continue ahead. Before I forget, I grab my phone and send Penny a message.

Fancy going wedding dress shopping on Thursday?

Since Mum and Dad will be here, I've taken Wednesday to Friday off work. Mum will want to join us, no doubt. I'll check if Avril can spare some time too. If I time it well, perhaps Bella can be available online.

Penny's reply is almost immediate.

I'd love to! Name the time and place.

Stopping at a crossing, I press the pedestrian button and type a reply while I wait.

I don't have the details yet. I'll send them tomorrow.

I set a reminder on my phone to make this a priority tonight once I'm home. A shiver of excitement ripples down my spine. I'm planning a wedding! I skip across the road when the little man turns green.

A couple of blocks later, I arrive at Le Salon du Clair de Lune. Situated on the ground floor of the Haussmann-style building, the entrance is adorned with elegant signage. Warm light spills out onto the street in the early evening. Two bistro-style tables and chairs are set up on the path, but they are empty.

Stepping inside, warmth envelops me. Removing my gloves and scarf, I shove them into my handbag. Soft music plays from the pianist on the grand piano in the far corner. The décor is in brown, gold, green, and crème, with subdued lighting from single candles in the middle of tables with plush chairs on either side and two chandeliers.

Geez this is swanky, but it's also welcoming and cosy. Nothing like the pubs in Australia. Then again, this is a cocktail bar, not a pub.

I spot Jacques and Rémy at a table, heads nearly touching as they talk in hushed tones. I've always seen resemblances between them, but when they're so close it's quite uncanny. Rémy is shorter and not as toned, his hair's lighter too, darker brown rather than black.

Laughter from the polished bar captures my attention and I turn to find Avril and another young woman, presumably Céleste, perched on stools and laughing over cocktails. Scrap that, it's definitely her. In appearance, she's a spitting image of Angélique with the same upturned nose and that regal air. Céleste looks a little worse for wear though with messy hair, makeup streaking down her cheeks, and a red nose from too much crying.

Today must've come as a big shock for her, but it's nice that she and Avril are bonding.

Jacques and Rémy are still deep in conversation when I approach. They don't notice me at first. It's only when I stop beside the table that they glance up. Rémy smiles a hello then reaches for his beer. Jacques jumps to his feet, embracing me and pressing his lips against mine.

"*Bonsoir beauté*," he says when he pulls back, the dimpled smile I love so much lighting up his face. "Would you like to join us? I can pull over another chair."

"No, it's okay, I'll join Avril and Céleste at the bar."

As if on cue, there's a gasp and Avril exclaims, "Jane, you're here!"

I send an apologetic smile to Jacques and Rémy then turn around as Avril lunges at me with an embrace. I cop a mouthful of brown hair as she titters in excitement. I have no idea where this girl gets her energy from. Actually, tonight it's probably from the alcohol.

"I'm so glad you made it," she loops her arm through mine and drags me to the bar and Céleste.

I'd hoped to at least gather my bearings first, but it's out of the frying pan and into the fire.

"Céleste, this is Jane." Avril gives me a gentle shove. "Your soon-to-be-sister-in-law."

I say gentle, but it's firm enough that I stumble and have to grab the bar to steady myself. I manage a quick glare at a smirking Avril before turning to Céleste whose head is bowed over a bright pink cocktail. She lifts it to peer at me. Her eyes are glassy, but she stares. Hard. I swallow the lump in my throat and breathe in deeply to calm my racing heart.

"*You* are Jane?" she asks as though we weren't just introduced. "Jacques'...*fiancée*."

Her nose wrinkles as she says it.

"It's lovely to meet you, Céleste." I hold out my hand, but she ignores it.

She sips her drink then turns to me, sitting ramrod on the stool. There is so much of Angélique in that icy gaze. She scrutinises me up and down, settling on my eyes.

"Maman told me you were plain." She sniffs and reaches back for her glass, taking another sip.

Sighing, I slide onto a stool, my heart sinking to my feet. Here we go again. This is getting old. Is this Plain Jane thing going to follow me *forever*? I raise my finger to get the bartender's attention.

"She was wrong." Céleste looks at me with a small smile. "You are very beautiful...for an Australian."

She finishes the last mouthful of her cocktail then lunges at me in an unexpected hug. She smells faintly of strawberries and something musky. Her arms are thin and bony. The hug is awkward, like she's not used to it. Hell, she probably isn't.

She pulls away as the bartender comes to take my order and she asks for the same again. I think she's had too much, but who am I to judge after what she's learnt today?

Despite the backhanded compliment, a smile fixes itself on my face. I'll take it.

"Thank you." I set my handbag on my lap.

"She was wrong about a lot of things." She folds her arms on the bar and rests her head on them.

"What are you drinking?" I ask when Avril sits next to me.

"I'm still going." She reaches for a glass of what appears to be whiskey and sips from it. "I'm from Scotland, I should be able to handle my liquor, but Céleste is drinking me under the bar."

Céleste groans and lifts her head in a semi-smile. I laugh despite myself, thanking the bartender when he places my cosmopolitan in front of me.

"You might have the DuPont blood, sister dear," Céleste says, propping herself up on her elbows to sip her refilled drink, "but you have not had to drown yourself in liquor for most of your life."

She giggles then starts sobbing over her glass. When I thought about our first meeting, I did *not* expect this. What am I supposed to do? I'm terrible at comforting crying people at the best of times.

"She does this," Avril whispers. "I just leave her to it."

"Right." Taking her advice, I turn to Avril. "How bad was it?"

"Well, *I* thought it went well, apart from me freezing up like an idiot." She rolls her eyes.

"You froze?"

"Totally, Jack had to step in, but it all sorted itself out."

"I am moving away!" Céleste declares, sitting upright and spinning around on her stool, swaying precariously.

When she sways too far one way, I lunge for her and slide my arm across her shoulders to keep her steady.

"Why are you being kind to me?" she asks, looking up at me through doe-like eyes. She appears so vulnerable and my heart goes out to her. I underestimated Céleste DuPont. Then again, I think Jacques did too. This is what comes from parents controlling their children to the point of never knowing one another.

"I barely know you," I answer. "I have no reason to be nasty."

"Yes, you do. I said some terrible things about you in the past."

I bristle at her words but I let them wash over me. "But you didn't say them *to* me, I'm sure I can let it slide."

"I was angry." She nods as though confirming this fact to herself. "I thought you were breaking my family apart." Tears trickle down her cheeks and she guzzles her full cocktail in one go. "Turns out you only showed my brother what a real family should be like." She hiccups and wipes her nose and eyes on the back of her hand. Suddenly she groans and her face pales. "Jane, I do not feel well."

I send a panicked glance to Avril. "Quick, I need your help."

Céleste heaves but holds a hand over her mouth, holding everything in. Frantically, Avril and I help Céleste to a bathroom close by. We make it into a stall just in time for her to fall to her knees and vomit up hours of alcohol.

No food either, by the looks of it. Ugh, gross.

"Ugh, gross," Avril whispers my same thoughts, holding her nose.

I try not to breathe through mine as I hold Céleste's hair back.

When she's emptied her stomach of what appears to be everything, she flushes and sits on the tiled floor with her knees pulled up to her chest, her skirt riding up, and starts sobbing. I can't leave her like this.

"Avril, can you tell Jack we have to go? Ask him to request an Uber. We'll have to take Céleste home."

"I do not want to go home!" Céleste wails.

"It's okay," I sooth, sitting beside her and sliding my arm across her shoulders, "you can stay with Jack and me." I gaze up at Avril who nods and rushes out of the bathroom.

"Why do you call him Jack?" Céleste asks with a sniffle.

I tell her the story, which leads to more stories of our last two years together. It's about ten minutes later before Avril returns, declaring the Uber has arrived, but Céleste is content leaning against my shoulder listening to me. She's a little girl in the body of a thirty-something woman. The DuPonts have so much to answer for. I only hope she can start a new life like her brothers have.

"Help me get her up," I say to Avril once I'm standing.

Together we assist a very drunk and emotional Céleste to the waiting car.

"Jacques, why did you not tell me you and Jane were engaged?" Céleste asks in English, a couple of minutes into the journey.

He glances back from the front seat, first at me, then at Céleste. I don't miss the guilt in his eyes.

"We were not speaking," he responds. "I'm sorry we did not have much of a relationship."

"It is not your fault. I made no effort either. But I suppose—" She sighs and gazes out the window then back at him. "We were never encouraged, were we?"

"No."

She leans forward to hold out her hand. "I am sorry too. Let us try to be better as brother and sister, yes?"

Jacques takes her hand and squeezes it. "I would like that."

Before turning back to the front, he catches my gaze once more and we share a smile. I see it in his eyes, the hope that maybe he hasn't lost his siblings after all.

Chapter 6

Jacques

I come out of the shower, one towel wrapped around my middle, and a second drying my hair. When I enter the bedroom, Jane stretches in bed and her eyes flutter open.

"*Bonjour beauté*, did you sleep well?"

She sits up and pushes her hair away from her face, the covers falling to her waist. "Very." Her voice is thick with sleep. "Why didn't you wake me?"

To me, she is the most beautiful first thing in the morning. Her satin pyjamas are twisted, there are adorable creases on the side of her face, and her eyes are bright.

"You are not working today, I wanted you to sleep longer." I sit on the edge of the bed and peck her lips.

She gets to her knees behind me, resting her arms on my shoulders and clasping her hands over my chest. Goosebumps rise on my skin when she kisses my shoulder and inhales deeply. "Mmm, you smell divine." She gives me a final squeeze then gets off the bed. After grabbing a change of clothes, she ducks into the bathroom.

"What time do your parents arrive today?" I call out.

"About lunchtime, I think. I'll have to double check."

I hear the toilet flush followed by the shower turning on a few seconds later.

"I feel bad that we're kicking Céleste out," Jane continues. "Are you sure she doesn't mind? She told me she understands, but what if she's just being nice?"

I go into the bathroom to finish drying off. "She wouldn't *just* be nice," I say as I hang up my towels. "She may be having a few revelations, but she is a DuPont first and foremost. One of our biggest failings is speaking before thinking."

Jane grins at me through the shower glass. "Ah, so you admit it's a trait?"

"I do not deny it, but I am working on it." I wink at her, leave the bathroom, and go to the walk-in wardrobe to pick out my clothes for the day. "Besides," I say louder so Jane hears me over the water, "Céleste said last night she will go travelling." I select a suit, shirt, and tie from the rail, then walk back out and start changing.

Céleste has been staying with us since Monday. I have enjoyed spending time with her, but she is still prickly towards me. Not as bad as it once was, but we have a long way to go. We can talk civilly and have meaningful conversations, but she is still in denial.

She does not believe Maman knew everything about what Papa did. She claims we are blaming her unfairly, arguing that knowing about Aimée's non-disclosure does not confirm Maman knew the full details. While I understand her point, there is still no solid proof confirming or denying this. Besides, the fact Maman is in hiding speaks volumes to me, but not to Céleste. This is why we cannot move past it.

The shower switches off. "Céleste travelling, huh?" Jane asks.

"To 'find herself'," I add as I tie my shoelaces. "Whatever that means."

Céleste and I stayed up late last night talking over drinks when she told me this.

"I get it," Jane says. "She's been lied to, manipulated, emotionally abused, and primed to be something she may not be."

I hum in response, letting this thought sink in as I go out to the kitchen to start on coffee. She makes a valid point. Did I not have to 'find myself' at one point? For the same reason? Having been controlled and manipulated for so long, apart from my business venture, I had no idea who I was.

Jane enters a few minutes later dressed for the day, her hair hanging in damp tendrils around her shoulders. She removes items for breakfast and places them on the centre island. I place a mug in front of her when she slides onto a stool.

"Thanks." She takes a sip.

"Thank *you*. You reminded me that I was once in Céleste's position. I understand what you mean now."

Jane beams as she grabs a bowl, filling it with granola, fruit, and yoghurt. I turn back to start on my coffee.

"Have you given any more thought about your groomsmen?" She asks a couple of moments later.

"Yes." After pouring hot milk into my mug, I place it on the centre island. "I will ask Claude to be my best man and Rémy and Hayden as groomsmen. I have not asked them yet, though. I will do that later."

Since hiring Hayden as the Regional Manager of the Australian office, he has become more than a valued staff member. He is a good friend. One I would be proud to have stand beside me on my wedding day.

"Hey, that's perfect!" Jane's eyes light up. "I can pair Claude and Penny, and Avril and Rémy together, that will just leave Hayden and Bella. They're both single, right? They live in Surfers too, and they're similar age…" she trails off and waggles her eyebrows.

I chuckle and shrug. "Why not?"

Jane grins and eats a spoonful of her breakfast. Céleste comes out of the spare room, yawning as she shuffles over to the counter still in her nightgown.

"Coffee?" I ask her.

She mumbles a, "*Oui s'il te plaît,*" as she slides onto a stool next to Jane.

I turn back to the machine.

"I hear you're thinking of going travelling," Jane says to Céleste.

"Might as well do something," she says in English. "I will not have a job for much longer, right Jacques?"

I turn back and frown at her. "What do you mean?"

"Rémy told me you are merging the companies." She scoffs and picks up a blueberry, popping it in her mouth. "Did you think this through? All those people who will lose their jobs?"

I cock my head to the side. "What makes you say that? A merger does not necessarily mean that. I hope to be able to keep most of the staff."

I almost add 'the trustworthy ones' but this may not go down well. This is something I will discuss with Claude and Rémy.

"Besides," I continue, "the will states you and Rémy must have positions with Entreprises DuPont and that will transfer over with the merger. Your job is safe, Céleste."

She rolls her eyes. "Lovely to know I *only* have a job because the will states I must."

"I did not mean it like that." I sigh and finish making her espresso, placing it in front of her. "Even if—"

"Do not worry, Jacques, I am still going to travel and will resign from my position when the time comes. You do not have to worry about me." She stands and picks up the small cup. "Excuse me, I will enjoy my coffee in bed."

I sigh again and sit on a stool opposite Jane, taking a long sip from my coffee. I glance at Jane who smiles sympathetically.

"Give her time, Jack." She reaches across to squeeze my hand. "She's still very bitter, and for good reason. Just be patient."

I reach for a bowl and pour in some granola and add yoghurt. "I understand, but it is frustrating. When it comes to the family or her job, she takes everything too literally. I wanted to tell her even if not for the will, I would have given her one."

"I know." She pulls her hand back and finishes her breakfast. "And I'm sure she knows too, deep down. I think travelling is a great idea for her. Maybe we should offer her our apartment for a bit in Surfers? We're still paying rent, so it might as well be put to good use."

"Yes, that is a wonderful idea. Just don't forget to warn her about the weather."

Jane chuckles and nods.

I finish breakfast, kiss Jane goodbye and rush to work.

T he first meeting of the day is via video conference with the key stakeholders of Entreprises DuPont and Solutions Exécutives, to discuss how to proceed with the merger and any objections. I am expecting some pushback, after all this is Papa's legacy. There are still a few people around who worked closely with him and may be averse to the changes.

To my surprise, even though they voice concerns and ask questions, there are no objections. There is no enthusiasm at all. They have lost all passion and motivation. Perhaps this is going to be for the best. I am confident their staff and my staff combined will make Solutions Exécutives even greater.

When there is a unanimous agreement that the merger will go ahead, the next step is to go over the financials. This is my biggest concern. If it is very bad, it could be a big hit for my company. Then again, with Papa's unexpected lump sum due any day, that will help.

I stay online with Rémy when everyone else leaves. I want to go through the financial figures together before sending them on to the accountant. As we do so, I immediately see one glaring issue.

"Why did you never tell me there was so little follow-through? The incoming business is great, but there are very few results."

It explains why Rémy has not been able to move the company forward.

He flushes. "Why do you think I want out? I am not cut out for this."

This is what comes from not showing enough interest. Even though I taught Rémy what he needed to know, I left him to run Entreprises DuPont alone because I wanted to focus on my own business. Doing so means I inadvertently let him sink or swim.

"I'm sorry I did not make myself available to you after I mentored you," I say.

"It was not entirely your fault. I could have come to you, but I chose not to. For so long I thought this was what I wanted, but when I did not care about the lack of results, I realised I needed more from life. I am not a businessman like Papa...or you."

"What do you want to do?" I close the financial documents.

Rémy shrugs. "No idea, but it is probably a good thing. We have a lot to cover for the merger. How long do you think it will take?"

"I am unsure. Most likely a matter of months, but there are too many factors involved that may or may not slow this down. Do not let it stop you from thinking about what you want to do though. Céleste says she is going to travel, maybe you should too."

He pulls a face. "No, thank you. I do not have any interest in travelling."

Yet another thing we have in common, although my views have changed over the last couple of years. Travelling is much more appealing when Jane is with me.

Rémy frowns and his gaze moves to a second screen.

"What is the matter?" I ask.

"I have received an email from Céleste." His eyes move as he scans it. "She is quitting from end of business today and has a flight booked for this evening to Australia." He purses his lips. "Did you know she was leaving so soon?"

I shake my head. "I told her we needed the spare room for Jane's parents, but I assumed she would go back to her place until she made plans. Jane said she would offer her our apartment in Surfers Paradise, but I did not expect anything to happen yet."

My phone vibrates on the desk next to me. Unsurprisingly, it is a message from Céleste.

Thank you for letting me stay in your apartment in Australia. I accepted Jane's invitation and will be leaving tonight. I have emailed Rémy my resignation. You no longer have to worry about me.

Céleste

"Will you be okay without her?" I ask Rémy, putting my phone aside. "If you need someone, we can hire a temp."

He rakes a hand through his hair. "No, do not bother. We will manage." He mutters something under his breath then louder, he says, "I must go," and logs off.

With a sigh, I reply to Céleste.

You are welcome, though I wish you had given more notice. I did not expect you to leave so suddenly. You have put Rémy in a difficult position.

After sending the message, I email the financial information to the accountant and by the time I am done, Céleste has replied.

There is nothing to keep me here. I will apologise to Rémy, but I cannot stay in this city another day.

I stare at it. How can I be angry at her? I understand all too well the need to escape. I type back one last reply.

I understand. Safe travels, and do not be a stranger. You are always welcome here.

With that sorted, I return to work. There is not much else I can do with the merger until I get a reply from the accountant.

Next, I ring Tavish. I speak to him and Aimée together, asking how their business is going. They report all is going well and I email them an exit form to sign that will end our contract. It is always thrilling to witness a business succeed, but it is even more so this time because of *who* it is. It is almost as though I have, in some small part, repaid her for her kindness during my childhood.

At ten a.m. my phone rings. *Maman?* Why is she calling now?

I pick it up and swipe the screen. "Yes, Maman?"

"We must talk, Jacques. There is information you do not know."

"About what?"

Silence then, "I would rather not talk about it on the phone."

I breathe in deeply and release it. "Fine, but it cannot be this week." I can probably find time, but I am doing things on my terms, not hers.

"Fine. Tell me the time and place and I will be there."

The phone beeps as she hangs up. Well, that is a first. She is answering to me for a change.

Chapter 7

Jane

Thursday morning the intercom buzzes and I run up and press the button. "I'll be right down," I say to Penny who is visible on the screen display.

I suggested she meet me here so I can talk to her on the way to the bridal store without anyone overhearing. We'll meet everyone else there. Bella said she'll be able to join us online for a little while before she goes to bed, so I'll call her when we arrive.

Mum and Dad arrived yesterday and it's so great to see them again. They were both jetlagged, and Mum appeared quite peaky. This morning she has more colour and seems perkier, so I'm trying not to let it bother me. Still, there's no hiding the niggle in the back of my mind. I can't help it after everything she's been through.

They went out early to have breakfast and start exploring the city on foot. We're supposed to be meeting in an hour, at noon, to visit the first bridal store and we'll have lunch later. Dad will meet Jacques at his office and, along with Claude and Rémy, will be having a 'boy's lunch', as he put it.

I've given Mum and Dad the relevant addresses and directions, but it'll be interesting to see if they get lost. The metro is easy to navigate, and they only need to read the street names, not pronounce them. Still, Paris is a far cry from Adelaide.

Grabbing my coat, I don it then pick up my handbag and rush down the stairs. Pushing on the door, I burst through to a waiting Penny and grin at her.

"*Bonjour*!" I greet her in a singsong voice, hugging her.

She laughs and hugs me back. "Someone's chipper this morning."

"I'm going wedding dress shopping, what did you expect?" We link arms and start walking. "So," I draw in a breath, "how are you?"

She glances across at me, eyes narrowed. "I'm fine, why do you ask?"

A shiver ripples down my spine as a lazy, cold wind tunnels down the road. "Because it's a normal question friends ask each other. But—" I pause then confess, "Claude *did* ask me to check on you. Said you were struggling with something." I shrug. "I've been so busy and I've been a bad friend, so I wanted to check in anyway."

Penny deflates and she unlinks her arm from mine. "Bloody Claude."

I frown. "What's that supposed to mean? He's just worried about you."

We turn a corner and she throws her hands up in the air, automatically speeding up in her frustration. "I said I was fine, but he doesn't know when to quit." She huffs. "I told him not to tell anyone. I have no idea what to do, Jane. I've got two kids already. Do I really want a third?"

"Whoa, hold up." I stop and grab her arm, forcing her to stop too. "What the hell are you talking about, Penny? You're...you're *pregnant*?"

Her eyes widen as her face pales. "I...I thought that's what he told you."

"He just said you might need a friend."

"Oohh." She covers her face with her hands. "It wasn't meant to get out." She drops her arms and her eyes are brimming with tears. "I don't think I can do it again, Jane." Her bottom lip wobbles. "I love Amélie and Henri to death, but I never wanted a third child."

My instinct is to lighten the mood with a joke about breeding like rabbits, but I'm pretty sure it's not the right time.

"So, what are you thinking?" I ask instead.

"I told Claude we should keep it quiet until after the first trimester, but honestly," she blinks when a couple of tears drip down her cheeks, "I'm thinking of...of terminating it and telling him I miscarried."

I gasp, catching the attention of some people passing by. "Penny!" I stare at her, my mouth opening and closing. I shake my head and hasten to add, "Of course it's your choice, but *lying* to Claude?"

She tries to wipe away her tears, but this only makes way for more. Sighing, I dig around in my bag for a travel packet of tissues and hand them to her. She takes one out and wipes her eyes.

"I know, I *know*, it makes me a terrible person. But, Jane," she grabs my hand, the soggy tissue wet against my palm, "he's *so* excited. How can I tell him what I'm thinking?" She lets go of my hands and starts pacing. "Hell, it kills me to even think it. I'm not like that, but I don't think I can do it."

"Penny." When she paces back to me, I grab her by the shoulders and force her to look at me. "I understand your train of thought, I do, but Claude's the father and he deserves to have a say in this too."

"It's *my* choice," she says with a sniff.

I release her shoulders and sigh. "Yes, of course it is, but he should still know. If you don't tell him and go through with it, one day he'll find out and it'll ruin your relationship. You guys are so strong, don't go there."

She stares at me through tear-filled eyes but manages a jerky nod.

"You need to think about this, and you must talk to Claude about how you're feeling. But I'm always here if you need someone else. You don't have to do this alone, okay?"

She gives me a watery smile and we embrace.

"Now." I step back. "Are you ready to go shopping?"

"Wait, have you even set a date yet? If, and I mean a big *if*, I keep this baby"

"Don't worry about it. We can plan it either before or after the baby. If it comes to that, of course."

She pulls a face. "You can't plan your wedding around *me*. Maybe I shouldn't be your Matron of"

"Wash your mouth out! You're not getting out of it that easily."

She finally smiles properly, and I swear a smidgen of hope fills her eyes. "You're a good friend, Jane."

I grin and loop my arm through hers once more. "I know, now come *on* already, I'm desperate to find my perfect wedding dress!"

Penny and I gasp as we approach La Belle Mariée, a three-storey Haussmann-style building. There are two ornate windows on the ground floor adorned with wrought iron accents and stunning bridal gowns in each window.

The entrance is an arched dark wood double door, embellished with intricate carvings of vines and roses. Flanking the entrance are two lamp posts with delicate scrollwork and floral embellishments. A hand-painted sign sits above the door displaying *La Belle Mariée* in elegant calligraphy.

"I never thought a bridal store could look so beautiful." I'm not sure why I'm whispering. Tears well up in my eyes at its beauty.

"I'll say one thing," Penny also whispers. "Be glad Jacques is loaded."

I swallow and nod, starting to doubt my decision to come here. I saw pictures online, so I knew what it looked like, but up close...wow. I remind myself of the budget I set. I've allowed a decent amount for the dress, without being stingy. It may be tempting to buy the most expensive one, but I must be firm. For me if nothing else.

"Jane."

I spin around to see Mum arriving. She stops and gasps. "Oh, what a beautiful building!"

Avril turns the corner and waves, grinning and breaking into a run. We embrace then she stands back and gawps. "Holy crap, check out this place!"

"You guys go in," I say. "I'll dial Bella in."

After connecting her and showing her the exterior, I keep my phone up so she can experience everything as I go inside. Of course, the interior does not disappoint. The brightly lit area makes everything appear so clean and...*white*. The walls are covered in delicate wallpaper with floral patterns and a crystal chandelier hangs from the ceiling. The floor is covered in plush, champagne-coloured carpet. A spiral staircase to the left, adorned with wrought iron railing, leads up to the first level.

There are mannequins wearing gowns, and rows of dresses line the walls. At the back are a row of large dressing rooms with full-length mirrors and curtains pulled to the side. There's a modelling stage in the centre, and soft music fills the air.

"*Bonjour.*" An elegant woman appears from upstairs. "*Comment puis-je vous aider?*" She asks how she can help us.

For a moment I'm awestruck by this woman. She. Is. Stunning. Looking to be in her fifties, she's the epitome of elegance. In a way she reminds me of Angélique with her perfect posture and Parisian attire. The silk pantsuit and antique jewellery would give Angélique a run for her money.

The biggest difference though is this woman exudes warmth and welcome with a friendly smile and sparkling hazel eyes. Her chestnut brown hair is streaked with grey and pulled back in a chignon.

Penny pokes me in the ribs and my mouth snaps shut. Oh my goodness, I haven't been gawping at her like a fool this whole time, have I? Ugh. How embarrassing.

"Uh, *Bonjour,*" I stammer, suddenly forgetting how to speak French. Clearing my throat, I add, "Do you speak English?"

The woman nods and clasps her hands together. "*Oui,* I do. Who is the bride-to-be?"

"That'll be me."

"*Magnifique,* you will make a beautiful bride."

My cheeks turn warm as a smile stretches across my face. For once, I'm not Plain Jane.

"I am Madame Sabine and I will assist you. Are these lovely ladies in your bridal party?"

"Yes—"

"Jane," Mum calls, interrupting me. "Come and look at this."

I smile apologetically at Madame Sabine, hand my phone to Penny and join Mum at a rack of dresses. The one she's holding out is stunning.

When Madame Sabine joins me, I say, "This is my mum, and this," I point to each in turn, "is Penny, my Matron of Honour, and Avril and Bella are my bridesmaids. Bella is in Australia."

"Lovely!" Madame Sabine clasps her hands in front of her chest and beams. "And this dress," she goes over to the one Mum is holding out, "is *superbe*." She rakes a critical eye over me then back to the dress and nods. "*La mère de la mariée* has excellent taste."

Mum peers at me in question.

"Mother of the bride," I translate.

"*Oui*, I apologise, I forget my place." Madame Sabine takes the dress off the rack. "I will hang this in a dressing room. Keep looking, keep looking."

She walks off, taking two more off the racks as she heads to the dressing room.

When she returns, I ask, "Do you sell bridesmaid dresses too?"

"*Oui*, upstairs on the second floor."

I turn to the girls. "Why don't you start looking for bridesmaid dresses? Someone will fetch you when I try something on. Bella," I turn to the phone, "maybe you can check out dresses on your end?"

"What about the style?" she asks. "If you want them to match, you may need to grab it there. I can send you my measurements."

"I want you all to be comfortable. So long as you're all wearing the same colour, I don't mind what the style is."

"What's the colour?" Penny asks.

"No idea," I say, and we all laugh. "But you can look at what styles you like."

"Come with me." Madame Sabine gestures to the girls.

Avril and Penny chatter as they make their way upstairs with Bella still online, following Madame Sabine.

I turn to a rack to sift through more dresses when there's a *thump* followed by, "Oh!" from Mum.

I turn to find her on the floor, a couple of dresses splayed out around her.

"Mum!" I run over to her, take her hand, and help her to her feet. "What happened? Are you okay?"

"The dresses," she blusters, bending down to pick them up but stumbles again. I grab her just in time and steady her.

"Don't worry about them, let's find you a seat."

"Oh dear." She leans on me and limps as I lead her over to a stool. "I'm so sorry. I have no idea what came over me."

I hang up the dresses, relieved that they're okay, and go back to Mum, sitting on the spare stool next to her.

"Do you have a headache?" I ask, taking her hand.

Mum told me she will be more susceptible to headaches now after her surgery.

She forces a smile. "No, one minute I was sifting through dresses, the next my legs gave way." She chuckles and her cheeks turn pink. "I must still be jetlagged. I'm fine now."

I watch her critically, but she won't make eye contact. I'm still holding her trembling hand.

Madame Sabine returns. "Is the blushing bride ready to try on some dresses?"

Chapter 8

Jane

Confession time. I hate clothes shopping. I always feel so judged. But Madame Sabine has been fabulous, no judgment at all. I've tried on two lovely dresses, but not what I'm looking for. Now, I've just slipped into the third one and...Oh. My. Goodness.

I'm in love.

"How does the dress feel?" Madame Sabine calls from outside the changeroom.

I can't answer. My eyes are glued to the mirror, staring at this stranger in front of me. I never thought I could be so *beautiful*.

"Jane? Are you okay?"

I did not expect to walk into the first bridal store and find the perfect dress. I blink a couple of times and go to speak but all that comes out is a croak.

A chuckle sounds from the other side and in French she mutters under her breath, "She has found the one." In English she adds, "I will give you a moment."

I went for ivory rather than plain white since it's not as stark. It's simple but exquisite. It fits like a glove, hugging curves I never thought existed. With lace cap sleeves, the neckline is a sweetheart design. The bodice is adorned with lace appliqués, carefully hand-sewn in a botanical pattern of blooming flowers and delicate vines.

Flowing from the waist, the skirt cascades down in layers of soft silk chiffon and splays out on the floor in a small circular train. I turn to another mirror so I can easily view the back of the dress, its sheer lace panels framing a low V-shaped backline.

Tears sting my eyes as I turn back and grin at my reflection, running my hands over the silky material. This is the one. I don't want to go anywhere else.

Drawing in a breath, I reach for the lock and slide it across. Opening the door, I step out. Madame Sabine, obviously hearing me, appears within seconds and gasps, her hand flying to her mouth.

"*Oohh la la*, you are truly *stupéfiante*."

Breathtaking. She says I'm breathtaking.

"Come, come," she takes my hand and guides me out of the dressing room and onto the stage.

Mum and the girls turn, Penny still holding the phone with Bella online, and they gasp at once.

"She is stunning, *non*?" Madame Sabine gushes as she fusses about neatly positioning the train on the floor.

Mum bursts into tears then rushes up and hugs me so tight I can't breathe. It's a whirlwind of activity as the girls talk all at once. My face is flaming from the attention, but I can't deny I'm loving every moment. Isn't this what every girl dreams of? Finding their dream dress and feeling like a princess? This is a once-in-a-lifetime experience and it's *my* turn.

Mum pulls away and moves behind me, playing with my hair and holding it in various positions as she suggests styles. Madame Sabine searches for veils and shoes while the girls present different accessories—earrings, necklaces, and tiaras.

It's all so wonderful yet overwhelming and before long I'm a blubbering mess. They're happy tears, of course, which only makes everyone else cry. Including Madame Sabine. I swear she must have the happiest job in the world.

I don't glance at the price tag. When I told Madame Sabine my budget, she muttered something about the perfect dress not having one and I didn't dare bring it up again. Is she right? This is supposed to be one of the most important days of my life. Shouldn't I be able to splash out? I may only wear it once, but I'll be looking back on photos for years to come.

The silly thing is the only person standing in my way is *me*. No one else has stipulated what I should or shouldn't spend. *I've* put a price tag on it because I want to stay true to myself. But it's *one* dress.

I have a vision in my mind of exactly how I want my wedding to look, and the dress is perfect for it. If I hadn't already talked myself into it, I have now.

It'll be on the beach, the early afternoon sun warm on my skin. The chairs laid out on the sand will have ocean-blue sashes tied in bows around the back. The altar and archway will be decorated with a stunning array of summer flowers. The men in light, airy suits, the bridesmaids in light blue dresses. Amélie as a flower girl in a gorgeous light blue dress, scattering flower petals on the sandy aisle.

"Light blue," I blurt, silencing everyone who peers at me in question. "The bridesmaids dresses. I want them to be light blue."

Madame Sabine claps her hands in glee. "*Superbe*! We have many varieties of light blue upstairs."

My dress is a near-perfect fit, but Madame Sabine takes note of a few alterations around my unfortunate small bust, and I request a shorter train. By the time we leave I've got my entire outfit sorted, including shoes and accessories. I didn't expect to be this successful, but at least now I have more time to focus on other plans.

"I should go," Bella says from the phone. "Thanks so much for including me today."

We all wave goodbye and Penny hands my phone back to me.

Once on the street, Avril says, "I have to go too. I promised Ma and Da I'd help them in the shop." We embrace then she rushes off with a skip in her step.

"Me too," Penny says, touching my arm. "I've got to pick up the kids. Claude's Mum is looking after them." She gives me a weak smile and holds a hand against her stomach.

There is no missing the worry in her eyes and I embrace her, saying in her ear, "Talk to Claude. Please? Maybe consider a therapist too. There's help out there."

We pull away and I capture her gaze, waiting for a response. It takes a few seconds to come, but finally she forces a smile and a nod before turning and leaving. I'm not convinced she will do anything, and I'm tempted to talk to him myself. I don't want to go behind Penny's back, but she's not herself and I worry she's not being rational.

"Shall we go?" Mum asks.

I make a mental note to text Claude later then turn to Mum. "Sure. How about lunch and some sightseeing?"

Jacques

I probably did not need to make Maman wait until we met up, but there is a strange sense of power knowing I have the upper hand. It has been one week since she called, and I am off to meet her now before I start work.

With Liv and William holidaying in southern France for a few days, Jane and I are back in our work routine. Over the weekend we did some sightseeing with her parents and made some progress with the wedding plans. Even setting a date for December. Now we only need a location, but a date should make it easier.

I pause outside the agreed café and peer inside. I spot Maman at a table for two. She is sitting rigidly with her back to the door, folding and unfolding a napkin. Is she nervous?

I step through the doors and stop beside the table. Maman glances up.

"Oh, Jacques, *bonjour.*" She stands and kisses both my cheeks. When she pulls back, there are tears in her eyes. "It is lovely to see you. May I buy you a coffee?"

I nod and she goes up to place the order. Removing my coat and satchel, I hang them on the back of the chair then sit.

Maman returns and sits opposite me, her smile stiff. "Céleste tells me she is in Australia." She picks up the napkin and unfolds it. "She says the weather is very warm."

I pour us some water. "It is summer, so yes it will be."

She hesitates. "I see," she finally says, sipping hers.

"She mentioned you are engaged." She keeps her eyes averted.

"That is correct." I take a sip of my water to keep my hands busy.

She folds the napkin again and meets my gaze. "Congratulations. I am happy for you and...Jane." She forces out Jane's name and it irks me.

"Is it so difficult to say her name?"

She sighs and lays the napkin on the table. "I apologise, Jacques." Her smile is forced but more natural. "I suppose I am upset that I heard through Céleste. You did not tell me yourself."

"You have earned that right, have you?"

Her mouth opens and closes a couple of times before she drops her gaze and her shoulders droop.

I am tempted to forgo this farce and leave, but our coffee arrives so I stay seated. I take a long sip, hoping it will calm my frayed nerves.

"You said you had information for me," I say. "I do not have a lot of time. I must go to the office soon."

I check the time for effect—eight fifteen a.m.

Maman shuffles in her seat and sips her espresso. "Jacques, first I wish to...apologise." For this she meets my gaze. "I have let you down, and of course Rémy and Céleste."

"No, I think Céleste received everything she ever needed. She was always your favourite."

She stares at me hard, pursing her lips and nodding. "Yes, I suppose you are right. In some ways. When it comes to showing and bestowing emotions, I have let you all down. I have never known how to show...love." Her brow furrows. It is as though even now she cannot fully understand it.

When she shakes her head, a loose strand falls from her fancy up-do and she pushes it back into place. "Jacques, I do not wish to excuse my mistakes. I am only here to explain *why* it happened, which in turn will help you understand why I turned a blind eye to your Papa's many...indiscretions. Will you hear me out?"

She gazes at me with such eagerness, I cannot say no. Perhaps this will give me the closure I need. But what about the others?

I question this and Maman says, "Céleste I spoke to last night. She did not react well, so I will give her time. As for Rémy?" Maman shrugs. "He does not wish to talk yet. But that is up to him I suppose."

I raise an eyebrow. "Alright." I sit back in my chair. "I will listen."

A small smile kicks up one corner of her mouth. "Thank you."

She sits in silence for a moment, appearing to focus on her breathing. She takes a couple of sips of her coffee before she speaks. "Have you ever woken up one day and looked back on your life only to realise it is not what you thought it was?"

I stare at her in disbelief. This is deeper than I expected.

"In a way, yes," I answer. "Why do you think I started my own company? That was just the beginning. Then I met Jane and I saw a lot of what was not...right."

Maman stares at me, her eyes glistening. She dabs at them with her napkin. "I did not understand for a long time. Your leaving felt like a betrayal. But I understand now."

She sips her coffee. "When your Papa got sick and the doctors said it was terminal, we were upset as you would expect, but it did not feel real. The next morning, I woke up with a sense of relief."

I lean forward slightly. "Relief?"

She nods. "It was the knowledge that I would soon be free of a life of fear."

I fold my hands in my lap, surprised by this turn of events. Maman feared for her life? I reflect on that day in Papa's office a couple of years ago. The day Jane left Paris at the beginning of our relationship. Maman appeared afraid for a moment, but she concealed it.

"Your Papa was a domineering man. I learnt early in our relationship that I should never disagree with him." She purses her lips and shakes her shoulders as though blocking a memory. "That is neither here nor there now. All I am trying to say is I knew my place and disagreeing with him had consequences."

"You never tried to leave him?" I ask. "You could have taken us with you."

Her face turns hard. "I would have had nothing, Jacques. I had no one to turn to. I grew up in a life of luxury, marrying into it was expected. I had no skills. I would not have survived any other life. It was easier to shut down all emotion and ignore him. All he wanted from me was someone by his side at events and a son to take over the company from him."

"And that was me." The words are bitter on my tongue. "I was nothing more than a necessary piece of equipment to keep the family empire running."

She stares at me but does not answer. Not that she needs to, the truth is in her eyes. "Céleste was unexpected, but she gave me the happiness I craved."

And we all know about Rémy, the unwanted child. Of course, I do not say this aloud but I am sure she is thinking it.

"As I said, Jacques, I do not wish to make excuses. Nothing can make up for past wrongs. I only hope we can improve the future going forwards."

I say nothing. The truth is, I do not know if I can. It is too early to decide. I am sorry that she lived a life of fear. No one should ever have to endure that. But I am still so conflicted.

"And that is why you never spoke up about Aimée?" I say. "You knew everything, your signature was on that non-disclosure, but you did nothing. Out of *fear*?"

She gives a single nod, holding her head up high. "I regret that very much. I would like to speak to Aimée. Or Avril. Either would be fine. I am aware an apology will not fix anything, but I would like to give one anyway."

I sit straighter in my chair. "I will not give you their contact details. They want nothing to do with you."

Maman huffs. "I could easily find them myself."

"Why are you asking me then?"

"Because despite how it may appear, I respect you, Jacques."

It is a roller coaster of emotions this morning. She *respects* me?

I sigh and rub my temples. At the end of the day, it is not up to me, is it? I refuse to give out any details without their consent, but I cannot decide for them. The least I can do is talk to them.

"Okay, I will ask." My coffee is unfinished, but I stand. "I must go to work, but I will contact Avril and I will message you with an answer later today."

Maman stands also, hands clasped in front of her. "Thank you, Jacques."

I nod then turn and rush out of the café.

Chapter 9

Jacques

Jane rushes out to the kitchen and places her handbag on the counter, digging around in it. "Don't forget Mum and Dad are back today."

They have been in southern France for a week. They will stay with us for two more nights before heading back to London.

"I have not forgotten," I reply, removing a mug from the overhead cupboard. "Coffee?"

"No thanks, I'm meeting Penny before work."

Ah, yes, she did mention that last night. I nod and close the door, placing the mug under the nozzle of the machine for my coffee.

"Ah ha, here it is!"

I glance back at Jane who is grinning and holding up a piece of blue material.

"What's that?" I ask.

"The colour I've chosen for the bridesmaids dresses." She places it on the counter. "This is for you so you can match any accessories. Flowers, ties, that sort of thing."

I glance at it then back at her. "That should be easy enough, blue is an excellent choice."

Jane bites her bottom lip and glances at me with a furrowed brow. "You will take it with you when you go shopping, won't you?"

"It's blue," I say with a shrug, turning to start frothing the milk. "I will not need it."

I hear her gasp and I smile to myself as I bring it to temperature.

"Please tell me you're not serious." She stops beside me and grabs my arm, causing the milk to slosh over the edge. "Crap, sorry."

I put the jug frother down and turn to her, chuckling. "You are so easy to tease. Do not worry I will make sure the colours match."

She glowers at me, but I only grin and kiss her. "You should go. You do not want to keep Penny waiting." I pick up the jug and pour the milk into my coffee.

Jane steps back and buttons her coat before taking her handbag off the bench. "Hey, any chance you can have a chat with Claude today?"

I sip my coffee and peer at her over the mug. "Everything okay?"

She hesitates, shuffling from foot to foot. "It's not my place to say. Penny confided in me last week and she's going through something big, but I don't think Claude realises how much she's struggling. I thought about talking to him, but I think it might be better coming from you. I told her she should talk to him, but I don't think she has. I'm worried about her."

I nod and put my mug down. "I will try and speak to him today."

"Thanks." Jane comes up to kiss my cheek then waves as she rushes out the door.

As I drink my coffee, I think about what she said. I have noticed Claude hasn't been his happy self. I thought the constant merger meetings were wearing him down. I would not blame him, there is a lot of work involved.

Of course, there is no backing out now. I would not dream of it. Still, it is a big deal and something neither of us have done before.

My biggest worry is the financial aspect. The accountant promised to email me today, so I will know how we stand soon. Apart from that, my next concern is staffing. With Rémy's help, I need to get to know the staff at Entreprises DuPont. The last thing I want is to bring in people that will destroy the morale I have worked so hard to achieve. I must choose very carefully who I keep on.

Finishing my coffee, I leave for work. I would like an early start before the meetings of the day begin.

When I arrive and log in, there is already an email from the accountant. I open it and read through it with bated breath. She has given a detailed report on the financial pros and cons, along with her final recommendation.

Anxiety knots my stomach. The report is not great, but it is not the worst possible outcome either.

My company can wear it, and she says it will be a smart way to grow, but it will not be easy. We must have an excellent business plan in place, and I make a note to revise this with Claude.

I trust my accountant, she has proven her worth over the years, and if she says we can do it, I am sure we will.

Having the staff from Entreprises DuPont onboard will help but I am concerned about how people will adjust. It will be a massive transition that will take time.

Closing the report, I send a copy to all relevant stakeholders and organise a meeting to discuss our next steps. It is nine a.m. when that is done. I hear Jane's cheery good morning when she arrives, and that alone settles my anxiety.

In the beginning, we were nervous about spending so much time together. Would we resent one another? It is safe to say we do not.

We only have lunch together once a week, so we will often go days when we do not even talk in the office and will only see each other before and after work. We both agreed not to smother each other, and it is working well.

I am prepping for my nine thirty meeting when Claude knocks on the door. I glance up and one look at him tells me everything is *not* okay. He is not in business attire. Instead, he is wearing jeans and a t-shirt. His face is pale, and his hair is messy as though he has raked a hand through it too many times. I may not have to initiate the conversation after all.

"Can we talk?" He asks without a greeting.

I nod and he enters hastily, closing the door a little too hard. When he sits in front of me, he runs his hands down his face until they land in his lap.

"Are you okay?" I ask.

He shakes his head.

"Are you unwell?"

"Penny wants an abortion," he blurts.

I jerk back in surprise. He has missed some steps and not revealed everything, but it is not difficult to connect the dots.

"Wait." I sit forward. "Penny is *pregnant?*"

Claude nods. "I was so excited when she told me a few weeks ago. We agreed to keep it quiet for the first trimester, but just this morning, she—"

He stops on a sob and glances up at the ceiling as he exhales.

"She's not coping." He rests his hands on his lap. "She doesn't want a third child. Says she doesn't think she can cope." He rakes his hands through his hair, anguish written across his face. "I don't want her to do it, but I know it's her choice. I won't force her either way, but I don't want her to make a rash decision."

"Claude." I have no words. "I'm so sorry. What do you need?"

"To take some time off. Starting now."

And there it is. Of course, I will not deny it, I pride myself on always putting family first. It is just unfortunate timing.

"The timing is terrible," he continues as though reading my mind. "But," he clenches and unclenches his hands in his lap, "she's eight weeks pregnant so we only have a little bit of time before she must decide if she'll...go through with it." He puffs out a slow breath. "She needs help and I want to be there. We've always shared everything, but it is not enough anymore, so I must step up."

I nod. "Take all the time you need."

Visible relief flashes across his face and his hands splay out on his legs. "Thank you, Jacques. Really." He pauses and worries his bottom lip with his teeth. "I think she needs to see a doctor. I'm worried she may have depression. She hasn't been herself since Henri was born, but she's always pushed through. Any time I mention anything about mental health, she clams up. But it's getting worse."

"Seeing a doctor is a great idea. If she can get help to cope, she will be able to think clearer."

Claude nods. "Exactly." He leans forward in his chair. "I still want to help with the merger when I can. I won't be able to do my normal work duties but keep me in the loop with anything about the merger and I'll do what I can."

I nod and open the staff calendar. We have a short discussion and I enter one month of leave for him.

"You will tell us if we can do anything?" I ask as we stand a few moments later, and I go around to him.

He smiles now, looking less uptight. "Of course, thank you." He slaps my arm and squeezes.

Once he leaves, I sit back down. Being one man down is going to make this difficult. My heart does a little flip in my chest and the anxiety returns with force. I am happy Claude is putting his family first, it is what I want too, but I need to find someone who can take on his other duties.

Chapter 10

Jane

The sun is warm on my face as Mum, Dad and I sit outside a café with a coffee and croissant. I tell you what, I'll never eat croissants in Australia again. Unless they're traditional.

It's Wednesday and Mum and Dad are flying back to London this afternoon. I've taken the morning off so we can enjoy brunch together. I'll travel with them to the airport, then I'll go to work.

They spent a few days in London when they arrived, but they're returning for two days before flitting off to Scotland for a week, followed by Ireland for another week. I can't deny I'm a little envious, but I'm so glad they can do this. I'll have the opportunity when Jacques and I go on our own European honeymoon, which we've been planning. I can't *wait*!

Mum and Dad are in their own bubble, talking and smiling. I've been worried about Mum since she and Dad returned from southern France. She's having more headaches and has been unsteady on her feet. She brushed it off as tiredness, so they've lain low the last couple of days. Seeing her rosy-cheeked and happier today puts my worries at ease.

Leaving them to their own devices, I take out my phone and check my emails. I found a great venue in The Maldives for our wedding and sent an email yesterday, so I'm hoping to have a reply from them. We decided to settle on The Maldives in the end because it's such a popular location and there are so many islands to choose from. The all-inclusive packages are amazing.

The upside of using a venue is that their events organiser will take a lot of the planning off my hands. While I didn't mind doing it all, I won't complain if they take over.

When I spot a reply to my enquiry, asking to set up a suitable meeting time, my heart skips. With a grin, I type back a response and suggest this weekend.

"So." I pocket my phone after Mum and Dad finish their conversation. "Ireland is your final stop, right? What's the plan once you're home?"

They nod and Dad answers for both of them. "I think we need to rest for a while. Your mother has overdone it."

An icy breeze tunnels down the road, taking away the warmth of the sun. I shiver and pull my jacket tighter around my chest. It doesn't last long and the warmth returns.

I look at Mum hard, then turn to Dad. She might be looking better, but I think back to that morning at the bridal store when she fell over. "Are you two keeping something from me?"

The question is unexpected, but I realise it's been in the back of my mind for a while now. She just hasn't been herself.

"Don't be silly," Mum says, averting her eyes.

Of course, I don't believe her. I glance from one parent to the other, but they're avoiding my gaze. I sigh and fold my arms across my chest.

"Let's go for a walk," Mum suggests, looking at me with a too-bright smile. "We have time, don't we?"

I glance at my watch—ten thirty a.m. "We have about forty-five minutes until we should make our way to the metro station."

"Well then." She stands. "What are we waiting for?"

She sways and grabs the table. Dad jumps to his feet and steadies her by placing his arm across her shoulders.

"I think you should rest—" I start, but she ignores me and walks off with Dad holding her hand.

"Paris is such a beautiful city," she says over her shoulder. "It would be a shame not to enjoy it as much as we can."

Sighing in frustration, I reluctantly follow.

Walking through Paris may be one of my favourite pastimes, but today my heart isn't in it. For half an hour we walk and take in the sights. I'm hyperaware of Mum slowing down and she starts limping. She's flagging and I'm worried. Really worried.

We're passing another cafe when she stops, grabbing the back of a chair. "How about a coffee?" she says, panting.

Dad and I stop and glance at each other, then at Mum. Her cheeks are flushed but her face is pale.

"Mum, I think we should—"

"This café is lovely," she interrupts, pulling out the chair and collapsing into it.

Dad sits also and places his hand on top of hers, looking at her in concern. My worry spikes and I slide into another chair.

"Come on you two, what's going on?" I'm willing myself not to panic but not liking the look that passes between them. "And don't say 'nothing'."

Mum sighs heavily and rests her elbows on the table before cradling her head in her hands. I glance at Dad who looks afraid.

"You should probably tell her," Mum struggles to say.

I sit upright, my panic spiking from zero to one hundred. "Tell me what? What's going on?"

Dad is too stunned to say anything and Mum shakes her head. What does this mean? "I feel light-headed," Mum says. Despite the fact it's not at all hot, a sheen of sweat forms on her brow.

She's barely audible over the passing traffic, but I catch it and I jump to my feet. Rushing inside, I purchase a bottle of water and take it back to the table. Dad twists the lid open and holds it out to her. She appears to gain control and sits up with a slow, deep breath, taking the bottle and sipping from it.

When she goes to put it down, she can't set it straight. It topples over and water gushes out over the edge and onto the ground. I lunge forward to pick it up the same moment Mum groans and sways, toppling to the right. Dad jumps out of his chair to stop her fall, and I realise she's passed out.

"Mum!"

Dad glances back at me, panic-stricken. "Jane, call an ambulance."

"What?" My brain blanks out and all I can do is stare as she turns a concerning shade of ash. It slots into place and I grab my phone, dialling 112 with trembling hands.

The ambulance arrives and in less than an hour we're at the hospital. Dad is sitting on a hard chair while I pace back and forth, agitation tightening my stomach up in knots. I tried to ring Jacques earlier, but he didn't answer, so I left a message. He'll come as soon as he can, of that I have no doubt. I could've called the office and left a message with reception, but with so much merger stuff going on, I didn't want to bother him.

I don't mind though. I think I need this time to figure out what the hell is going on. Is it the brain tumour? Something else? Mum told me she was in remission and the doctor gave her the all-clear. She never said whether it could return, and I never asked. I suppose I was too afraid of the answer. Now I wish I had.

I stop pacing and turn to Dad. He's sitting with his elbows resting on his thighs, arms dangling between them and head drooping forward.

"Care to tell me what's going on?" I demand, taking the seat next to him.

He lifts his head slowly and deliberately like it takes a huge amount of effort to move. "Your mother didn't want you to know."

"Know what?" I run my hands over my legs, needing to do something to calm the anxiety.

He scrubs his hands down his face, looking contrite. "She was never going to make a full recovery."

I stare at him agog, the words hanging over me for a second before seeping in. *Never going to make a full recovery.*

Dad huffs out a sigh and grips his hair. "She's terminal, Jane. She had the surgery to give her time, not to cure her."

Panic washes over me. All this time, from the moment she sat in my kitchen telling me she had a tumour to now, they've both been lying to me. I even went to an appointment with her, but the surgeon only talked about the surgery and what was involved. Not the diagnosis. Having never been through it before, I didn't think to ask questions.

Am I so emotionally weak they had to hide it from me?

I'm trying to think of something, *anything*, to say but my mind is blank. My body turns numb, but my heart is racing.

"Jane—" Dad reaches out for my arm.

His touch awakens something inside me, and I jump to my feet, needing to move. "Wait." Everything slots into place. "You two have known this for *months*, led me to believe she was in remission, and yet this whole time she was..." My throat closes when I try to say the word and I gag on it.

Dying.

"You've got to understand—"

I turn on him, anger controlling every part of me. "No, I can't understand *anything*. You both lied! There is nothing that makes this right. I could've handled the truth, you know? I'm not some weak thing you have to protect."

Dad sighs and stands. When he approaches me, I take a step back. He holds his hands up and stops, nodding in understanding.

"It's not about protecting you." His arms fall to his sides and his shoulders droop. "You and Jack were starting your lives in Australia and your mother thought if she told you, you would've put everything on hold."

"Damn right I would have!"

"Exactly and that's what she didn't want. She wanted you to live your life, for you and Jack to find your feet after—"

"But it's *my* choice! Neither of you should've taken that away from me." A lump lodges itself in my throat and tears brim my eyes.

Guilt passes across his face and he shrugs as though saying there's nothing he can do about it. While he's right, I'm still furious.

The desire to flee comes on so suddenly, I can't think straight.

"I...I need air," I mutter, then spin around and rush towards the automatic doors.

They open as I approach and I speed through them, nearly colliding with Jacques arriving but managing to dodge him and break into a run.

"Jane!" he calls behind me. "What's wrong?"

I shake my head and keep running.

Chapter 11

Jacques

"Jane! What's wrong?"

She swipes away tears and shakes her head but does not stop. Her sob catches on the breeze as she dashes past and disappears between buildings.

I take two steps to follow, then change my mind. She needs time alone. With a sigh, I turn back to the hospital.

I had finished one back-to-back meeting and was about to go into another when I noticed her message. It was garbled and I could not understand much apart from 'Mum collapsed' and 'hospital' followed by an address. I left Hugo to cancel the rest, stating a family emergency, and came straight here. Liv and William *are* family. They are the loving and caring parents I always longed for.

I could have asked Claude to take over, but he has taken Penny out of the city for a few days.

The sound of doors opening and closing brings me back to reality. Blinking a couple of times, I realise I'm triggering the doors by standing in front of the sensor.

Drawing in a breath, I release it and go inside.

Cold dread ripples down my spine as I think of the endless possibilities of Liv's condition. Of course, the first thought is the brain tumour, but she was supposed to be recovering well from that. Something else? She has not entirely been herself. Tired, off-colour, unbalanced.

Jane running out crying has me thinking it is the worst-case scenario.

I follow the signs to the emergency room where William is sitting on a plastic chair with his head in his hands. I sit beside him and place a hand on his shoulder. He sits upright, a spark of hope briefly lighting up his expression. It disappears quickly and his face crumples.

"I thought Jane might be with you," he says.

"What is going on? Is Liv okay?"

He shakes his hand and tells me everything.

As it sinks in that she is not going to survive the tumour, iciness washes over me. It is no wonder Jane is so upset. I wish I had gone after her now, but I think being here is best. Perhaps if I can obtain all the information, I can share it with her when she comes to terms with everything.

But why the lie?

"I know what you're going to say mate," William says. "We should have been upfront. When Liv told me she didn't want either of you to know yet, we argued black and blue for days about it." He rakes a hand through his hair. "I confess I only gave in because—" His voice breaks and he clears his throat. "—I didn't want to argue with her knowing she had so little time left."

His Adam's apple bobs as he swallows to control his emotions. My heart goes out to him and I squeeze his shoulder.

While I empathise with him, hiding the truth from Jane was still wrong so I choose my words carefully before responding. "I understand, but it is still unfair to Jane. She would have wanted to spend as much of the last few months with her mother as she could. We would have changed our plans."

"I'm aware of that." William glances at me, his eyes shining with unshed tears. "When we were planning this trip, Liv swore she'd tell her the truth, but the wedding plans took over and she...didn't." He covers his face with his hands and groans into them. "This is a bloody nightmare." He drops his hands. "Do you have any idea where she went?"

I shake my head, fighting the urge to go after her. I should wait until the doctor has given an update. William told me it had been two hours since Liv was rushed into the emergency room.

"I think she needs time to come to terms with this," I say instead.

William nods, the expression on his face one of regret.

"I will see if I can find anything out."

As I do so, the emergency room door opens and a doctor comes out. She takes in the waiting room packed with people, before calling, "Collins?"

William jumps up, and I join him as we approach.

"I'm Liv's husband," he says.

She glances from William to me then back to him. Her face is compassionate when she says in an English accent, "Mr Collins, please take a seat." She grasps his arm and leads him back to the chairs. Once he's seated, she sits beside him and peers at me. "Are you family?"

"He's my son-in-law," he says before I can respond.

Despite the dire situation, a warmth spreads through me, almost making me break out with a silly grin, but I catch it in time. This is neither the time nor the place.

"I'm Doctor Wright and I have been with your wife, Olivia Collins. You were aware of her latest brain tumour diagnosis, yes?"

He nods. "The original surgery and treatment gave her time but it was always terminal."

Hearing it said so matter-of-factly sends a shudder down my spine.

"Correct," Doctor Wright continues. "I have spoken to the doctors in Australia and received copies of her results. It appears her tumour has grown and is causing new symptoms. It explains why she fainted today. She says she's been unsteady too."

He runs his hands along his trousers. "Where to from here?"

"Surgery is too risky. We could consider further radiotherapy, but even that—"

He shakes his head, a tear sliding down his cheeks. "We've already talked about this. She does not want to go through treatment again. She knew this was coming."

"But we didn't," I cannot help interjecting. "Do we not have a say in this?"

Doctor Wright folds her hands in her lap. I look directly at William but he only shrugs as though to say 'it is not my choice'.

"Can she go home?" he asks. "She would want to be comfortable."

"I'm afraid she is not fit for travel, Mr Collins." She smiles sympathetically. "If treatment is refused, she will be moved into the palliative care ward. Once she is settled, you will be able to visit her."

William sits motionless, hands on his thighs, anguish written across his face. I have no idea what to say or how to respond, so I switch to practical mode.

"Will she have her own room?" I ask.

She shakes her head. "I'm afraid they're for private patients."

"I'll pay for it."

"Jack—" William interjects but I hold my hand up.

"Please," I look Doctor Wright in the eye, "if she cannot be in her own home, she should be allowed to be comfortable in her own room. Money is not an issue."

"What about the insurance?" William asks.

Doctor Wright stands. "We will handle all of that. Anything not covered will be invoiced separately." She reaches out and squeezes William's hand. "I am very sorry, Mr Collins. Please be patient a while longer and someone will advise you when you can see your wife."

He nods but his face is pale, like he cannot believe it has come to this.

I cannot believe it either.

Doctor Wright disappears behind the emergency room doors, and I turn to William. His eyes are brimming with tears as he stares into space. As Jane likes to say, 'what's done is done' and right now William *and* Liv need us. I must focus on encouraging Jane to visit Liv, otherwise she will regret it.

I draw in a deep breath. "I must find Jane. I will try and talk her into seeing Liv, but please try and see this from Jane's point of view. She is very hurt."

I want to add, "So am I," but I do not.

It is not about me.

I barely notice William's nod as I turn and rush out of the hospital.

᠆᠈᠈᠈᠊᠈᠈᠈᠊᠈᠈᠈ ᠊᠈᠈᠈᠊᠈᠈᠈᠊᠈᠈᠈᠆

P aris is a large city, where do I start looking?

Jane could be anywhere. I send multiple text messages but when she does not reply, I call but it goes to voicemail. I understand she is upset, but she must know I will worry.

I spend two hours scouring the streets and cafés around the hospital with no success. Before going further afield, I go home to make sure she has not returned, but it is empty. I ring Rémy and Claude on the off chance she contacted either of them, but she has not.

It is getting dark by the time I stop and regroup. Pacing the floor, I try to think of where she may be. Perhaps she went somewhere special. But where? I do not know where she has been with Liv, so all I can think of are places we have been to together.

Deciding to start with Francette, I exit the apartment through the front door. I will go on foot, so I don't miss anything. But as I am turning to leave, my name is called. I spin around, my heart leaping when I spot Jane walking towards me. Even in the unnatural light of the streetlights her cheeks are glistening with tears. Her shoulders are slumped, and she is dragging her feet.

I run up and envelop her, relief, anger, and worry pouring out of me all at once. "Where have you been?" I demand a bit too harshly, pulling away and holding her at arms-length, scowling. "I have been worried about you. Anything could have—"

I stop mid-sentence when Jane's face crumples and she bursts into tears. I close my eyes and force myself to regroup and breathe. Now is not the time to lecture, she only acted how anyone would have in her situation.

"Come here." I gather her close to me and kiss her forehead. "I'm sorry, I did not mean to get angry."

She shakes her head against my chest, followed by a muffled, "I'm sorry too." She pulls away and pushes her hair away from her face, damp with tears. "Mum's dying." Her bottom lip wobbles.

"I know, I'm so sorry. I've got more news when you're ready."

She manages a watery smile. "Listen to you go on those contractions, Jack."

I smile despite myself and wrap my arm around her shoulders. "Now come on, let us go inside and I will fill you in."

Jane gazes up at me, fear in her beautiful blue eyes. "Not tonight, Jack. Please? Can we just eat in front of the TV and watch a movie?"

I stop and examine her. I want to argue and tell her she must know now, but I accept she needs time.

"Okay." I guide her to the apartment. "But only for tonight."

Chapter 12

Jane

I peel my eyes open and wince at the sunlight coming in through the curtains. Groaning, I use my arm to cover my eyes.

"Who opened the damn curtains?" I call out into the void even though no one's home.

It's the weekend but Jacques is at work this morning. *Ugh.*

"I did."

I shriek and sit up, heart racing. Glancing around, my eyes widen when I spot Avril standing in the doorway, hands on hips. Far out, what's she doing here? What if I was *naked*? I don't often sleep in the nude, but occasionally I do. Oh my goodness, can you imagine the horror?

"What are you doing here?" I ask, swinging my legs to the side of the bed, my feet touching plush carpet. "And why did you open the curtains? I wanted to sleep in."

And spend time with Jacques. But *that's* not going to happen.

The merger is going to take time but I'm already resenting how many hours he's spending at the office. He's late more often, and this is the first weekend he's gone into the office. The busier he gets though, the more it'll occur.

With Claude on leave to care for Penny, Jacques will have double the work to do.

I understand, I do, but...I need him.

A shudder travels along my spine and guilt weighs me down. Mum's in hospital. Dad is sleeping on a cot beside her bed. Jacques visits after work, which adds to his lateness. And I'm—

Avril interrupts my thoughts, much to my relief. "You can sleep in another day." She leans on the doorframe. "Today we are going shopping. I've found a great bridesmaid dress and I want to show you."

I wave a hand and lay back down, pulling the covers back over me. "Nah, you don't need me there. I trust you girls. I want you to be comfortable, just make sure the colour matches the swatch I gave you."

Closing my eyes, I sigh and relax on the mattress. This is where I want to be. But suddenly I'm exposed to the cool air as the covers are ripped off me.

"Avril!" I sit up and make a grab for them, but she moves them out of reach. "Give them back, I'm tired!"

I'm aware I'm behaving like a petulant child, but it's the only thing I can control right now. A lump of irritation forms in my chest and unexpected tears prick my eyes.

Mum is in hospital, and here I am avoiding her, acting like nothing is wrong.

These thoughts hit me like daggers, causing the guilt to grow. When I glance up, Avril is staring at me with pity in her pretty brown eyes. The guilt becomes overwhelming and the lump rises in my throat in the form of a sob.

"Please," I beg, my voice breaking. "I just...I need..."

I need my mum.

And that's all it takes for me to lose it as I start to ugly cry. Gut-wrenching sobs and unintelligible snorts as I sniff back tears. This is useless.

Avril sits beside me and slides her arm across my shoulders. "Alright, I confess. Jack asked me to come around."

Ugh. Of course, he did. Not that I blame him. I haven't been the easiest to get on with over the last couple of days. While he's tactfully mentioned Mum and how she's doing, I've pretended like nothing is wrong. The times he's suggested I visit, I've ignored him. It's like some defence mechanism kicked in and I hate it.

I owe him an apology.

And Mum. *Especially* Mum. I've deserted her while she...she's dying.

This only makes me cry harder and Avril squeezes my shoulder, making all the right soothing noises. She's acting way above her twenty-three years and I can see how much she's like Jacques. It's no wonder they're close.

I pull myself together and grab the box of tissues from the bedside cupboard, wiping my face dry. "I'm so sorry."

"Don't be," she says, moving her arm away. "Jack told me everything, but he wasn't sure how much you knew."

I wince and run my hand through my hair. "I know she's..." I draw in a deep breath, finding the courage to say the word. "*Dying.*" It's still so hard to say. "But I have no idea how bad it is." I stare at her with wide eyes. "I'm scared but I'm also angry. Why did she hide it from me?"

She squeezes my arm and jumps off the bed. "The only way you're going to find out is by talking to her. And trust me, being open will be like a breath of fresh air."

"Oh yeah? Says the voice of experience, hey?" I feel one hundred years old as I force myself to my feet and go to the closet to grab my clothes.

"I spoke to Angélique the other day, and—"

"You what?" I spin around, gaping at her. "Does Jack know about this?"

Avril rolls her eyes. "Of course he does. He's the one who asked me if I wanted to talk to her. She requested it and I said yes."

My mouth opens and closes, disbelief rendering me speechless. "Avril! After everything she's done! Is your mum aware?"

Her eyes flash and she folds her arms over her chest. "With everything going on in your life, *that's* what you're getting hung up on? While I appreciate your concern, I'd rather you not get involved. I know what I'm doing. I only wanted to say that talking to someone about what's on your mind can help. Speaking to Angélique did that. To me."

She tuts and with another eye roll, storms out of the room.

I stare after her, her words seeping in and feeding the guilt. Feeling rightly chided, I go to the bathroom. I'll apologise to her soon. For now, I must shower. Avril's right, I need to talk to Mum.

In the shower, I lean against the tiles as the hot water wets my hair and runs down my skin. It revitalises me and helps me think clearly for the first time since Mum went to hospital. I make myself consider the whole situation.

Mum sick. Dying. Stuck in Paris.

It must be terrifying for her. I'm sure she'd rather be home, but why isn't she? Is there a medical reason?

If I'd let Jacques tell me everything, I'd know.

I'm so angry with myself for punishing her. So what if she didn't tell me the truth? Yes, it's wrong and it hurts, *a lot*, but what's the point? All I've done is waste important time. Two days I could've been with her, and I wasted it.

Ironic, huh?

I push off the tiles and finish my shower in record speed. After blow drying my hair, I change and find Avril on the sofa, scrolling on her phone. She looks up and offers me an apologetic smile.

"Hey," she jumps up and slips her phone in her handbag, "you ready?"

I nod and we leave.

Out on the pavement, Avril says, "I'm sorry I snapped before. You're going through a lot and you don't need me doing that. I felt bad for your mum while you were ignoring her."

"It's okay." We start walking. "I deserved the wake-up call. You made me see it from Mum's perspective and it's time I stopped being selfish. So, thank you, I appreciate that." I link my arm through Avril's as we turn a corner. "I wasn't trying to get hung up on the Angélique thing. I was surprised, that's all."

"I understand and I appreciate your concern. Jack's acting all concerned too. He thinks she's going to manipulate me or something." She waves a dismissive hand and tucks her hair behind her ear. "But I'm not easily manipulated. Besides, I don't really like her. She's so…so…"

"Stuffy?" I offer.

"Yeah!" Her face lights up. "Stuffy, arrogant and superior. She thinks she's the Queen or something. I'm tempted to tell her this isn't England."

I snort a laugh. "I'd love to see her face." We stop at a pedestrian crossing, and I press the button. Spotting a bridal store across the road, I ask, "Were you still going to show me your dress?"

Avril squeezes my arm and grins. "Of course not. It was a ruse to get you to the hospital if you put up a fight."

I roll my eyes but laugh in disbelief. "Thanks, I guess."

I must thank Jacques later too.

➽➽ ⫷⫷

Avril leaves me at the entrance of the hospital and says she will come by next week. I'm nervous about going in alone, but I don't delay. I've delayed too long as it is. Once I've found out what room she's in, I go straight there.

My stomach knots up as I walk down the hallway towards it. The closer I get, the more my muscles tighten. Nausea washes over me. What will she look like? How sick is she? I wish I'd listened when Jacques tried to update me so I could be prepared. But this is on me, and I need to put on a brave face.

Her door comes into view and I slow my pace when voices drift out. Mum and…someone accented. Male, but not Jacques. French though. Maybe it's a doctor or nurse.

Stopping at the door but out of sight, I draw in a deep breath and hold it. Laughter sounds as I release it and I smile. I'm glad she's laughing. I hope it means she's doing well.

Stepping forward, I stop inside the doorway. The first thing I spot is the cot on the floor where Dad sleeps. He's not here and I have no idea what his schedule is. All I know is he's spent every day here. As I glance around the room, my jaw drops when I see Mum sitting up in bed. On a chair beside her is...Rémy?

Mum is bright and happy and *not* unwell. I can see her, she's got her head turned looking at Rémy. They're in deep conversation and don't notice me. They've met before, but I didn't realise they were so chummy.

While they're busy talking and laughing, I remain standing in the doorway, watching. Then I notice something even stranger. Rémy's in scrubs. Or at least something like it. It's a hospital uniform. Blue bottoms and a matching top with a visitor lapel badge.

Am I missing something?

There's a pause and Rémy glances up. "Oh, Jane, hello." He pulls his shoulders back, his face hard as he stares at me.

"Hi Rémy, hi Mum."

Mum whips her head around, a blinding smile on her face. "Jane!"

I run into the room and sit on the bed beside her while we embrace. A couple of tears drip down my cheeks and I breathe in her motherly scent. It's tainted with the antiseptic smell of the hospital and it rams home what's happening. She might look good but that doesn't change anything.

"I'm so happy you're here," she says when we pull apart.

"I'm sorry I didn't—"

She holds up a hand, silencing me. "*You* don't have to apologise, Jane. I do, and I am so sorry I didn't tell you the truth. I have a lot to explain, but—"

Metal chair legs scraping along the floor interrupt us. I glance up as Rémy stands. "I should go."

"Oh, Rémy," Mum reaches out for his hand and he gives it. "It was so good of you to visit. You're welcome anytime."

"Thank you, Madame—"

"Just Liv," she says with a laugh.

Rémy's cheeks grow pink when he smiles and nods.

"What's with the getup, Rémy?" I ask.

He peers down at his clothes as though forgetting but when he glances at me again, his shoulders are tense and his jaw twitches. "Nothing," he snaps. After a glance around the room, he says, "I must go," and rushes out.

Okay then. I raise my eyebrows at Mum. "What's that all about?"

"He's volunteering on the weekends as an aide of some sort. Visiting patients and the like. He's got an amazing bedside manner."

Huh. Well, there you go. Why is he being so defensive?

Shaking my head, I push that aside for now and turn to Mum. "Right, we need to talk. Tell me *everything.*"

Chapter 13

Jane

S itting next to Mum on her bed, my legs outstretched, I rest my head on her shoulder as I mull over our chat this afternoon. I'm up to date with everything and...I feel empty. Devastated. *Angry*.

I can't imagine life without her. She's always been there and it's unfathomable to me that one day she just...won't be.

"Are you okay?" Mum asks, running her fingers through my hair.

I cross my feet at the ankle and shrug. "Not really. There's a lot to take in."

She moves her arm to rest over my shoulders. "I know."

I blink away tears but it does the opposite and they drip down my cheeks. "Mum, I can't—" but my throat closes, and I can't finish the sentence.

Thinking the words is one thing, saying them aloud is a whole different story.

"Jane, shh." She squeezes my shoulder. "I understand how hard this is for you, and it's unfair because I've come to terms with it already."

"Well, that's not my problem," is what I want to say. I *could* have come to terms with it by now if she'd told me. Of course, I don't say it. But I'm struggling to let the anger and resentment go. I promised her I would, that I would do my best to make the most of what time we had left, but it's easier said than done.

As anger bubbles low in my belly, I clench my teeth and breathe slowly.

"It's very unfair," I say, keeping my voice even and void of accusation. "But I understand why you felt you had to do it."

I wince as I speak the words, hating that I lie. I *don't* understand. Not really, but I'm trying to, and I don't want to make this into a big deal. Now is not the time to be angry at her.

"Thank you." Mum smiles in relief.

Glancing out the window, the late afternoon sun shines through. "How about a walk?"

It's been dreary and chilly the last few days, so the sunshine is a welcome relief even if it's still cold.

She follows my gaze, smiling wistfully. "I'd love to, but I'll need the wheelchair." She gestures to it in the corner.

I swallow the lump of emotion in my throat. Her stability is worsening each day. She can walk but not far in case she falls. The chair is more for her safety than anything else. Unfortunately, as the tumour grows her ability to walk, talk, and function will worsen.

Shaking the thoughts from my head, I slide off the bed and wheel the chair over. Even though Mum gets into it with ease, I'm fully aware of how quickly it will change.

My mind is in a whirl as I push her down the hallway towards the elevators. There's got to be some way to ignore this niggling resentment and enjoy these moments with her. I'm not sure how yet, but I'll figure it out.

Once outside, I breathe in the fresh, cool air and it helps to relieve some of the emotion trapped inside. The bubbling anger begins to subside but is replaced with overwhelming sadness. Not much I can do about that.

I push the chair along a brick path through a garden with patches of grass, shrubs, and trees. As the sun lowers in the sky, it shines through the low-hanging leaves, casting dapples of light on the ground. Cement flowerbeds line the path, but being winter there are no flowers. I imagine it will be beautiful in spring.

We walk for a few moments in silence, passing other patients and visitors sitting at wrought iron table settings. It's not a big garden and by the time we reach the end, the sun has disappeared behind buildings and the breeze turns chilly. Mum shivers and crosses her arms, so I turn the chair around and make our way back to the doors we came out of.

When we're back inside, something occurs to me and I gasp, coming to a stop.

"What's wrong?" Mum looks up, her brow furrowed.

Grabbing my phone out of my jeans pocket, I groan when I notice the missed call and messages.

"I was supposed to be chatting to the wedding planner at a hotel in The Maldives. I forgot about it." I start typing back an apology email, and to ask when they're free next, then stop and glance at Mum. "Actually, would you like to join me on the call? I can try and organise something for tomorrow afternoon."

Mum's eyes light up. "If we're talking about wedding plans, do you even have to ask?"

I smile at her. "Duly noted." I finish the email then tap send.

On one hand, it feels wrong to be planning a wedding when everything is so dire. On the other, it's a sure way to keep our minds off the situation. And Mum wouldn't want me to change anything.

I pocket my phone and grab the wheelchair handles. "Let's go back inside, then I'll see if they've replied."

A smile remains fixed on Mum's face as we navigate the hallways. When we exit the elevator on her level, Mum says, "Thank you. I appreciate you taking me out. Maybe we can do this more often?"

"Of course." I squeeze her shoulder. "What's the likelihood they'll grant you a day pass?"

"As long as the doctor approves it and we take all the proper precautions, it should be fine. I'll ask her when she comes by next."

I nod as I start thinking about things we can do. Doctor Wright hasn't told us how much time Mum has left, but I am going to do better at making the most of whatever there is. If I can make up for some of the lost time, it might help shift this resentment.

When we arrive back at her room, Dad and Jacques are there and they're both surprised to see me. Jacques' surprise changes to relief and I smile sympathetically. I haven't made his life easy, but I owe him so much. *He* made the effort to visit Mum, despite how busy he is.

"Jane." Dad rushes over to embrace me.

I can only imagine how hard this has been for him. Not only was Mum rushed to hospital and told her time is limited, but he also had so much to deal with. Flight cancellations and refunds. Cancelling any other plans or accommodation. Dealing with the insurance agency. Talking to the Australian embassy.

I should have been helping him.

"I'm so glad you're here," he says when he pulls away, his eyes shimmering with tears.

"I'm sorry—" I start to say but he hugs me again, squeezing the words out of me.

"No more apologies. You're here now, that's all that matters." He steps back, a watery smile on his face. "There are some things I could really use your help with though."

I nod. "Of course, Dad."

While he turns to fuss over Mum and help her back into bed, I go over to Jacques and wrap my arms around him. He presses his lips to mine in a loving kiss.

"Thank you," I say when we pull away. "Your plan worked."

He grins, his dimples on full display. "You are not annoyed?"

"No, just thankful. I'm sorry I've been so difficult."

"Do not be sorry, I understand."

He embraces me, making me feel like everything is going to be okay. I still don't know how, but somehow.

Jacques

On Monday morning I arrive at the Entreprises DuPont building to meet with Rémy. I will spend the week here so he and I can discuss each staff member and their skillsets. We have meetings lined up with everyone so I can get to know them. I want it to be an informal chat, not a job interview or assessment.

If I can help it, I would prefer not to lose anyone. Over the last few days, we have worked out we will need everyone on board. But if anyone proves to be a bad fit, I will do what needs to be done.

Stopping in front of the building, which is so familiar to me, it is strange to think one day it will not exist in this form. The Entreprises DuPont signage will be gone and all that will be left is a memory of what once was.

I reach Rémy's office at eight thirty a.m. and he is already at his computer, a frown creasing his brow.

"What's worrying you?" I ask as I walk in, placing my satchel on a chair.

Rémy jerks his head up. "You frightened me. It is nothing important, just a petty staff complaint. Shall we grab a coffee?"

I nod and we make our way to a café next door. While we are waiting, Rémy is in another world.

"Everything okay?" I ask.

He blinks and shakes himself. "Yeah, fine."

The barista calls out our names. We pick up our order and make our way back to the office.

"Jane said she saw you at the hospital on Saturday. It was nice of you to visit Liv." My small talk to lighten the mood has the opposite effect.

Rémy tenses. He grunts and shrugs in response but doesn't say anything. I leave it alone for now.

Back at the building, we go into Rémy's office and shut the door. He sits in his normal seat and I sit opposite. Our first meeting is not for another few minutes, so I stretch my legs and loosen my tie. It is irritating me earlier than usual today. It appears being with Jane has made me relaxed in more ways than one. I do not enjoy wearing a suit as much as I used to. I wear it out of habit, not comfort. Maybe it is time to mix it up a bit.

"I wish to study medicine."

Rémy's voice cuts through my thoughts and I blink at him in confusion.

"I would like to be a nurse. Or a doctor." He sits up straight, his shoulders tense. "I am unsure what yet. I just want to do something...good."

This is a surprise. The family business has been such a big part of our upbringing, I never imagined Rémy studying anything else. What can I say? One moment he is saying he does not know what to do...now this.

"I have made up my mind." Rémy's eyes turn hard. "You will not make me change it."

Realising I have been staring at him, I pull myself together. "Sorry." I sit up straight. "It surprised me, that is all." I shake my head and smile. "Rémy, this is a fantastic idea."

He stares at me through narrow, suspicious eyes. "You really think so?"

"Of course, it's brilliant. Why would I try and change your mind?"

He smiles now, his shoulders sagging. "Maman and Papa said it was stupid. Told me being in the family business was more reputable. I was worried you might act the same way. I always knew I wanted to do this. It is why I am resigning. I did not say anything earlier because I was unsure how you would react."

This irritates me more than it should, but I say nothing. I cannot blame him for thinking it, so I will not make it a problem. There are still many areas where we are trying to find our feet on.

"I am not like them," I say. "They are wrong. I'm proud of you."

A smile spreads across Rémy's face and I swear there are tears in his eyes, but he blinks to hide the evidence.

"As much as I will miss you, you should do what you want, not what is expected."

Rémy relaxes in his chair. "Thanks, *frère*."

There is a knock at the door and he jumps up, turning to me with a bright smile. "Let's get this underway. No time to waste now."

He rushes to answer, a skip in his step.

Chapter 14

Jacques

I should have known it was all too easy. The merger was going too well and falling into place. It was only a matter of time until something went wrong.

"We have another one," Rémy says.

I glance up from reading an email, frowning. My stomach drops when his words sink in. "Another resignation?"

Rémy nods, turning the screen so I can read it.

I rake a hand through my hair. "*Merde.*"

"Effective immediately." He says it so dismissively.

It is Friday and after a week of meeting staff, we have ten resignations. Uncertainty sets in place as I think of all the possible reasons why. It cannot be because of Rémy's management, otherwise he would have seen a pattern before now. They have only started this week. How can I not take it personally?

Rémy and I have kept all communication open and honest, ensuring to keep them updated on the process and the timeline, so everyone is aware of what is going on.

Yet for some people this is still not enough.

"Why are you not worried about it?" I ask my brother.

Rémy shrugs. "Is it such a terrible thing?"

"Yes!" I place my laptop on Rémy's desk and stand, pacing the floor. "We need these staff and more, remember?"

Rémy sits back in his seat, hands behind his head.

"We should have a staff meeting today," I add. "There is too much uncertainty and people are clearly uncomfortable with me, or the merger."

"It is not necessary, trust me."

"I appreciate your optimism Rémy, but—"

Rémy sits forward, folding his arms on the desk. "Sit down, Jacques, please. Your pacing is unsettling me."

Grunting, I do so but my knee starts bouncing.

"You met the ones who are resigning, what did you think of them?" Rémy asks.

I shrug. "They were okay I suppose. They had a lot of experience, but not very memorable."

"Exactly. They were also the ones who worked closely with Papa. Who would let questionable decisions slide and turn a blind eye to everything he did. Why do you think they are leaving? They know you will not be like him."

My eyes widen and my knee stops bouncing. "I see your point, but how can we justify losing their years of experience?"

"We hire more people to replace them."

I open my mouth to object, but Rémy holds up his hand.

"Hear me out. Today's resignation is the only one effective immediately. We can deal with that loss. The other nine have given us four weeks' notice. Why do we not go through our previous applications and see who is still available to join us? You might have some at your company too."

I nod and exhale. "Yes, that may work. If we tell them about the merger, it might encourage them to come on board. People quite often like coming on when things are changing as they are more likely to make an impact."

"Exactly." Rémy's eyes twinkle.

"But." I deflate as I think about the never-ending workload ahead of us. "This is only giving us more to do." I run my hands down my face.

"Can Claude help? Did he not say he still wanted to be involved? Looking through applications should not interrupt his vacation too much."

I nod again. "Yes, that is a good idea."

Rémy turns back to his computer. I reach for my laptop when my phone vibrates on the desk next to it, so I take that instead. Claude's name displays.

"Speak of the devil," I mutter.

"What was that?" Rémy asks.

I wave him away. "Nothing." I swipe the screen and read the message.

Are you free? I need to talk to you.

Anxiety clenches my stomach. I do not like the tone. "I'll call Claude now," I say.

Rémy nods and I leave the office. Going into an empty meeting room, I tap on Claude's number.

"Is everything okay?" I ask when he answers.

"Yes," he says slowly.

I breathe a sigh of relief. "How is Penny?"

There is a pause.

He is silent for too long. "Claude? Is Penny okay?"

He sighs, then, "Yes, she is. She's making progress, but she's fragile. Look, Jacques, this isn't ideal but—"

"Go on," I coax.

"I'm going to have to go part-time. I need to be here to give her extra support."

This does not answer whether she is keeping the baby or not, but I do not push. He will reveal all when the time is right.

I release my breath thankful it is nothing worse. "Is that all? That will not be a problem."

"Are you sure? It's not right to be a partner in a business if I am not full-time. If you want me to—"

"No. You will always be my business partner."

"Maybe you should have a bigger percentage? Seventy-thirty perhaps?"

I rub my forehead. "Claude, I appreciate what you are suggesting but it's not necessary. At least not yet. Let us get you working on your new schedule, and we will think about other things later if it comes to it."

"Alright, but I'm not letting it go. We will talk about it when I'm back in a couple of weeks. Are you sure you're okay with this?"

"Yes, of course. I assume it will begin from when you return?"

"If it is no hassle, then yes."

"Okay. There is one other thing."

I ask for his help with the applications, and he agrees.

After we hang up, I pocket my phone and rub my temples. I meant what I told Claude, I do not have a problem with him going part-time but it does put more pressure on the business. I stand and go over to the window, glancing out over the city. The sun is hidden behind clouds today, but there is no snow.

I think about Hayden. He could help from Australia, but it will be easier if he is in the same time zone.

Turning away, I go join Rémy and after filling him in on my call with Claude, I say, "What do you think about bringing Hayden over for a few weeks? An extra set of hands will help."

He nods. "I agree, but who will manage the Australian office in his absence?"

I sit down and stretch my legs, crossing them at the ankles. "Samantha, the supervisor working under him, will be able to handle it."

"I think it is a great idea." Rémy glances at his computer. "How about some lunch?"

"Give me five minutes, I want to send Hayden an email first."

I do just so, requesting a time to chat so I can talk to him about everything. After it's sent, Rémy and I make our way downstairs.

I have enjoyed working with him this week. Working on the merger in general is drawing us closer as brothers. The divide that has been between us since we reconnected is lessening. I will be sad when he leaves, but I am also happy that he has found a path he wants to follow. A purpose in life.

"Have you heard from Céleste?" Rémy asks as we exit the DuPont building and step out onto the street.

"She texted me last night."

We have been texting semi frequently and our relationship is gradually improving. She apologised for not believing the truth about Maman knowing what Papa did. She said she has not spoken to her for a while, needing some time to figure things out.

When Rémy and I stop outside our lunch spot, I take out my phone. "Look at this." I show him the message and photo Céleste sent me.

The photo is of Céleste standing in front of an expensive campervan. She is tanned and appears relaxed.

"She is going on a road trip?" Rémy asks after he reads the message.

I pocket my phone and we go inside. "Yes. She is travelling around Australia. She said driving on the other side of the road has been an experience."

I remember my own experience of having to adjust. I am still not very confident and prefer to walk or let Jane drive.

"Great." Rémy's tone is bitter.

We find seats and I glance at him. "Are you jealous? I thought you said you didn't want to travel?"

He frowns. "I am jealous, but I do not understand why." He shakes his head in confusion. "Maybe it is because she knows what she wants to do."

"And you do not? You only told me on Monday about your venture into medicine. Does that not count?"

Rémy glances up from perusing the menu. "I suppose so, I just feel a bit stagnant because nothing is moving right now. I can only volunteer on the weekends, and I cannot start studying yet as there is not enough time."

"But you have a plan. Can you not enrol for a semester later in the year? Things will come together with the merger soon, and we will not have to work so much. Then you will be able to volunteer more."

A small smile tugs at Rémy's lips as his shoulders slacken. "Yes, I suppose you are right. Thank you."

We pick up our menus. Once we have decided, go up to place our order.

I am so happy for my siblings. They are finding new lives for themselves. Will Maman ever find a new path?

We have not spoken since our meeting at the café when she asked to speak to Avril. But I have been wondering about her. Avril is keeping me updated on their chats and apparently Maman is contrite. A part of me does not want to believe it, but I trust Avril.

I hope Maman can move on. I still do not know how, or even if, I will forgive her. We may never have a stable relationship, but I want her to be happy. I have never known her to be and that must be a miserable life.

Once seated again, Rémy takes out his phone and starts scrolling. I take out mine too and send Maman a message.

Would you like to have coffee?

―――⟫⟫⟫ ⟪⟪⟪―――

Sunday morning my alarm blares at five a.m. and I roll over to turn it off. Jane mumbles in her sleep and rolls over but does not wake. I lean over to kiss her shoulder then slip out of bed quietly and make my way to the bathroom.

I did not work yesterday and probably should be working today but have vowed to take the *whole* weekend off. I have told Rémy to do the same. He said he might try and do two volunteer sessions. I will have to work more weekends soon, but while Liv is still mobile, I want to spend time with her while I can.

Jane and I spent the day at the hospital yesterday. Today I am surprising them with a day out. Over the past week, Liv deteriorated quickly. She is becoming more reliant on a wheelchair or walker. This may be the last opportunity for her to enjoy the outdoors and Doctor Wright has cleared her.

We were recently advised that Liv has a matter of weeks left at most. A permanent knot sits in my stomach at the thought of losing her. Jane is struggling with it too, but she is putting on a brave face. My brave, beautiful Jane.

My heart is heavy as I step under the warm needles of the shower. I sigh and lean my head back to wet my hair. Everything is happening too fast.

I am so relieved that getting Avril to help Jane had the intended result. I was worried that I overstepped but she was appreciative. As much as I want to always be the one to help fix Jane's problems, it is not always possible. Sometimes it is a job for someone else. Sometimes they are not fixable.

Showering quickly, I step out, dry myself and change. I leave a note for Jane on her bedside cupboard, telling her where to meet and what time, then set her alarm to go off at seven a.m.

Chapter 15

Jane

I wake up with a gasp and jerk into a sitting position when my alarm blares, my heart racing.

What the actual hell?

Fumbling for my phone, I turn the alarm off and shake my head. Why would I set the alarm for seven-freaking-o'clock on a Sunday morning? Running my hands down my face, I'm about to snuggle back under the covers when a piece of paper on my bedside cupboard catches my eye. Aside from a book or two, it's always clear, so this is unexpected.

Reaching for it, I unfold it.

Bonjour beauté,

I hope you will forgive me for the early alarm. Meet me downstairs on the street at 8am. Wear something warm. I have a surprise.

Je t'aime.

Any annoyance I had disappears and my heart goes back to its normal rate as a smile stretches across my face. A surprise? Grinning, I push the covers back and scramble out of bed, rushing to the bathroom.

I *had* noticed Jacques was busier than usual. He didn't even make it to the hospital last night. Mum didn't mind though, so maybe she expected it. Now it all makes sense, she must be in on it.

While I shower, I go through everything it could be. A picnic on the Seine? A day trip or an overnight getaway? Somewhere in the country perhaps. We've been talking about spending a day or two in Champagne.

Excitement skitters along my skin as I step out and wrap a towel around myself. I don't care what it is, I'm just happy to be doing something together.

I'm ready half an hour early so I grab a coffee and drink it while pacing the apartment to ward off the excited energy.

At 7:58 a.m. I put my cup in the sink, make sure I have my phone and purse then rush downstairs. I push open the door and step onto the cobblestone street at exactly eight a.m. I peer up at the sky, which is clear but still tinged with darkness as the sun is only just rising. I breathe in the chilly air, filling my lungs with its freshness, and bury my hands in my coat pockets.

My breath comes whooshing out when a sleek black limousine pulls up outside the building. Seconds later the front passenger door opens and Jacques steps out. My jaw drops.

I gasp and clasp my hands together. "What's all this?" I run up to him and fling my arms around his neck.

Gosh it's great to be so...*free*. It may only be for a few minutes. Or maybe just today. But I want to embrace it.

I peer inside and meet the eye of the middle-aged chauffeur. He ducks his head, greeting me with a friendly '*Bonjour*' and a tip of his cap.

"Isn't he supposed to open the door?" I quip in a whisper to Jacques. "Are you taking over his job now?"

He glares at me deadpan but his lips twitch as he opens the back door. "Get in," he says with a roll of his eyes.

I giggle and duck into the back of the limousine, stumbling to a stop when I spot Mum and Dad already seated.

Confused, I turn back. "What's going—" but the door closes, cutting me off.

When Jacques has settled in the front, he turns his head and says, "You will find out shortly. Just enjoy the ride."

Baffled but excited, I make my way to the long bench seat and sit beside Mum, grinning at her and Dad. Mum beams at me in return. She's so *alive* today. Dad throws me a smile but he doesn't look as thrilled. Poor Dad. This whole trip has been so stressful for him. I helped him with some visa paperwork, and we met with someone at the Australian consulate. Everything is sorted on that front and now we...wait.

I shake the thoughts from my head. "What a surprise! Were you two in on this too?"

"Jack wanted to surprise us," Mum says. "In the end he could only surprise you, since Doctor Wright had to clear me to grant a day pass."

As the limousine starts moving, Mum turns to stare out the window. Leaving her to it, I move to sit beside Dad who appears to be a little glum. "Hey, you okay?"

He nods, his gaze fixed on Mum. His Adam's apple bobs in his throat when he swallows. Then he swallows again, and I realise he's trying not to cry. I loop my arm through his but say nothing, giving him time.

"Is this too much?" I ask quietly so only he hears. I don't want Mum to worry about him, and I don't want Jacques to think he's overdone it. It's clear why he's doing this. He wants us to make happy memories, but it's also a harsh reminder of what's looming.

Dad turns to me, his eyes cloudy with unshed tears. He blinks them away and manages a smile, shaking his head.

"Not at all. A little overwhelming maybe. Being fawned on like this, that is. But I think it's bloody wonderful what Jack is doing for your mother."

"For us," I correct. "He's doing it because he cares about all of us."

Dad pats my knee. "You've got a good bloke there, Jane."

I glance at the front of the limo where Jacques and the chauffeur are talking, but I can't hear what they're saying. I take in his profile, thankful he's in my life.

"I know." A lump forms in my throat. I love him so much, the thought of losing him terrifies me. It gives me a brand new perspective on the situation Dad is in.

I glance across at Mum. The smile hasn't left her face as the limousine continues through the streets of Paris. Before I can think, I find myself saying in a low voice, "Dad, what's going to happen after..." I shrug, not knowing how to say it.

It's probably the wrong time and place but I can't stop the words tumbling out. We haven't talked about the prospect of her dying. It's like we can't speak the words because it's impossible to imagine life without her.

She's the super glue that keeps everything together.

Whether now or later, we need to discuss it.

Dad's shoulders tense and he shudders. His jaw twitches as he glances at Mum, his eyes clouding over again. I bite my tongue. Ugh. I'm such an idiot. I definitely should've opted for later. It's supposed to be a happy day.

"Sorry," I mumble when Dad moves his arm away. "I shouldn't have asked."

I go to move but he places his hand on top of mine, stopping me. I glance back, a tear sliding down each of his cheeks.

"It's okay," he says, also keeping his voice low. "We can't bury our heads in the sand forever, can we?"

I shake my head.

"The thing is," he shrugs, "I don't know."

"Jack and I are still planning to settle on the Gold Coast once everything is sorted here. You can come and stay with us."

He shuffles in his seat, running a hand over his head. "You're a good girl, Jane, but you two won't want to put up with your old man."

"You're not that old, and we wouldn't mind."

Even though we haven't spoken about it, I know Jacques would agree. The last thing either of us want is to leave Dad alone and suffering in his grief.

Dad's face clouds over. "Thanks, Jane. Let's see what happens, shall we?"

That sounds suspiciously like burying his head in the sand, the one thing he said we shouldn't do, but I don't say anything. It was unfair of me to ask him that today. I gaze at Mum again who's oblivious to our conversation. We'd kept our voices low on purpose, but she's so transfixed she probably wouldn't have heard us if we were talking normally.

We fall into silence, and I move back to sit next to her, needing to be near her. Tears sting my eyes and my jaw hurts from clenching my teeth. Now the conversation is stuck in my head. What *will* life be like after she's...gone? I can't even begin to fathom it.

With the way she's deteriorating, she won't even be alive for my wedding.

This thought makes me shudder. When we chatted with the organiser at The Maldives hotel, Mum and I were so caught up in the plans, it never once occurred to me. Everything is booked, deposit paid but now I'm wondering...was I too hasty?

Stop thinking. Enjoy the day. Everything will work out.

Yet as I force myself to gaze out the window where the Eiffel Tower is standing in all its elegant glory, I wonder if it's true.

How is it possible for everything to work out?

⋙ ⋘

By the time we arrive at our destination, I'm over my melancholy and am cheery again. I'm determined to enjoy today and not stress about anything. I've been doing so well not overthinking things, and I can't go backwards now. Things have a way of working themselves out, right? Right, and I need to remember that. It's time to pull support from the people around me, not push them away.

Once we're out of the limousine, Mum in her wheelchair, Jacques leads us to a grassy area only metres away from the Eiffel Tower. Even after all this time, it still impresses me. It's by far my favourite Parisian landmark.

Jacques turns to us, his smile so wide and boyish it raises everyone's spirits. It's like a collective weight lifts off us all at once. With the sun shining, birds chirping, and butterflies fluttering around new flower blooms, spring is not far away.

"First stop, *petit-déjeuner*," he announces, stepping aside to reveal a picnic blanket and basket laid out on the grass behind him.

"What did he say?" Mum whispers behind me.

I spin around with a grin. "Breakfast," I translate.

"Oh, good!" Dad strides over and plonks himself in one corner. "I'm starved."

Mum rolls her eyes playfully. "I feel so forgotten when it comes to food."

"Sorry!" He goes to stand but I stop him.

"It's okay," I say with a laugh. "I've got this."

I push her a bit closer and with Jacques' help, we settle next to Dad.

Jacques and I sit opposite and he drags the basket across.

"This is perfect." I bump his shoulder. "Thank you."

I have so many questions about how any of this is possible, but I choose not to ask. Jacques has money and with money you can pretty much get anything you want. He's gone all out with great intentions and there is no way in hell I'm going to rain on his parade. The fact he's done this off his own back, out of *love*, only makes me fall in love with him even more.

Jacques glances across at me. "You think so?"

I nod and lean up to peck his lips. "Yes." I really can't wait to marry him. And it's not about the money. It's never been about that. It's all about the man he is and who he's become. There's just so much to love.

"Let us eat." He opens the basket and pulls out the picnic items—croissants with butter and jam, Quiche Lorraine, brioche, a variety of pastries, and juice and coffee to top it off.

"You've outdone yourself, mate." Dad rubs his hands together and reaches for a croissant.

"If this is all you've got planned for today, it's a winner," I whisper.

He grins at me, then we eat in silence for a few minutes.

When Mum and Dad are talking, I turn to Jacques and stare at him, overwhelming love washing over me. "I love you," I whisper, grazing my lips across his stubbled cheek. "Thank you so much."

He lifts my chin and gazes deep into my eyes. "*Je t'aime*," he says and brushes his lips against mine, a shudder traipsing down my spine.

When I move away and spot Mum and Dad staring at us with silly smiles on their faces, my cheeks flame. Clearing my throat, I pick up more food and casually ask, "So, what else do you have planned for today?"

Jacques tuts good-naturedly. "That would be telling. You must wait for the surprise."

Chapter 16

Jacques

Planning a day out for Jane and her parents seemed like a good idea at the time. I wanted to give them every opportunity to spend as much time together as they could. Organising it while juggling work *and* the merger? Not my smartest decision ever, but I have no regrets.

Over the past two years, I have been more careful with what I spend my money on. This is thanks to Jane mostly. But for this moment I have not held back. After all, it's for people I care about, not me. Not having to worry about money made organising it easier.

After the picnic breakfast, the limousine takes us to Musée du Louvre where I organised a personal tour guide to show us around the most famous paintings. Art is not normally my thing and during my whole life in Paris I have never visited, but today I am impressed. Even William, who did not appear interested at first, has been captivated by the enthusiastic guide.

After a light lunch on a Seine cruise, followed by a scenic tour of the city, our final tourist stop is the Arc de Triomphe. I promised to stay with Liv, while Jane and William climb to the top. We have already explored around the monument, and now she is content to sit in her wheelchair under the arc, staring at the inscribed names of all the French victories and generals.

"I'm not afraid of dying, Jack," Liv says, breaking the comfortable silence that settled between us.

Startled, I glance down at her only to find her smiling in contentment.

"I'm happy with the life I've lived," she adds, her voice barely audible over the traffic buzzing past. "I have no regrets."

I crouch beside her, so I am at eye level and better able to hear her.

"But I'm worried about Jane and William." She frowns. "Especially William. I have no doubt Jane will be fine."

We share a smile. I am relieved she trusts that I will look after her daughter.

"You do not need to worry about him." I place a hand on her arm. "We will look after him too."

She places her hand on mine, squeezing it. "Thank you, Jack. You're a good man." After a final squeeze, she releases my hand. "William and I always hoped to have a second child, a son, but it never happened." Her eyes are bright and happy when they meet mine. "I'm so glad you're part of our family now."

I open my mouth to say something, but a lump rises in my throat and words die on my tongue. My mind goes blank. 'Thank you' doesn't seem enough but it is all I am capable of.

I stand to stretch my legs, blinking away the tears stinging my eyes.

Liv yawns, then shivers when the sun disappears behind clouds that have been building up over the day. Worried she may have overdone it, I say, "Do you wish to go back? I have one more event planned, but I can cancel it."

"Don't you dare! I appreciate everything you've done today. I'm fine and I don't plan to miss out on the grand finale."

⤞⤞⟫ ⟪⤝⤝

The 'grand finale', as Liv put it, is dinner back where we started. La Tour Eiffel. I have booked a private area at the back of the restaurant where we enjoy a quiet, three-course French feast as a true family. When dessert arrives, the thought that this might be our very last meal as a family crosses my mind.

My heart sinks to my shoes. If the others are thinking the same, they are concealing it well. I blink away unexpected tears and zone back into the general conversation around the table. William is talking about Australian football, but it is lost on me.

When the night ends, we pile into the limousine once more. Liv and William are dropped off first, then Jane and I are taken home. I have joined her in the backseat, and we are sitting in companionable silence, her head resting on my shoulder as she swipes her phone screen, looking through the many photos we took today. It has been a successful but busy day. Knowing Liv and William enjoyed it makes me proud.

Jane puts her phone away. "Thank you for today." Jane lifts her head to look at me. "Mum and Dad loved it so much."

"And you?" I ask.

She smiles and nods. "And me. I can never repay you for this."

"I do not want any repayment. I did it because I love them and you."

"Well then," her smile is mischievous, "I suppose there are other ways I can repay you at least."

The sparkle in her eyes is nearly my undoing. Thankfully it is a short trip, and we make it home by seven p.m.

Jane and I are in each other's arms within seconds and stumble to our bedroom. Making love tonight is more passionate somehow...more intense. We fall asleep soon after, exhausted after a big day and high on emotion.

Monday morning comes around and my alarm blares at four a.m. The early night means I slept for a solid eight hours and I feel rested. I shower and leave quietly to pick up Hayden from the airport. I am expecting him to be jetlagged, so I plan to drop him off at the apartment and let him have a day to explore the city or rest.

However, when we are back in the car and driving to the apartment, Hayden is wired and wide awake.

"Nah mate," he says when I tell him my plan. "I'm raring to go."

I glance at him sideways. His hair is sticking up at all angles and his eyes are wide and bloodshot. "Are you sure?"

"Yeah, of course I am." He grins at me and lowers his head to glance out the window and get a full view of La Tour Eiffel still lit up.

It is still dark. The sun will not rise for another hour or so.

Hayden whistles in appreciation. "Nice."

"You have never been to Paris?"

He shuffles in his seat. "Nah. Been to a few places in Europe but never made it here. So what's the go? I'd like to hit the ground running. The busier I am today, the better. I'll sleep like the dead tonight but tomorrow I'll be good to go again."

I fill him in on the latest and explain the situation with Claude. I make sure to have total transparency across the whole management team. Since he is filling in for him, he must understand everything.

We arrive back at the apartment at eight a.m. and Jane is already awake and showered.

"Hayden, hi!" she greets cheerfully. "Did you have a good flight?"

"Great to see you, Jane," he replies. "The flight was pretty good. Hey, do you mind if I have a quick shower?"

"Of course! Jack will show you where it is."

I nod. "I'll show you to your bedroom first."

"Would you like a coffee when you come out?" Jane calls.

"Yes please," he replies. "I'll be living on the stuff today. Any chance I can have it on an IV drip?"

Jane chuckles. "Sorry, no can do."

I incline my head and Hayden follows me to the spare room.

Jane and I both agreed that he could stay here until we know when William will come back. Right now, it looks unlikely it will be any time soon. He is content at the hospital with Liv. Hayden is aware of the situation and happy to move if anything changes. Rémy has even offered his spare room if it's required.

Once Hayden is unpacking and showering, I go back out to Jane and wrap my arms around her waist and kiss her cheek.

"*Bonjour beauté*," I whisper, grazing her ear with my lips.

She shivers and spins around, wrapping her arms around my neck. "Good morning. Sleep well?"

"Very."

She grins but it slips when she steps out of the embrace. "Jack, I've been thinking."

I step back and lean against the counter, resting my hands on it. I nod for her to continue.

"Mum isn't getting better..." her voice breaks. She bites her lip and glances up at the ceiling as though pulling herself together. "...I know I should probably talk to you about this during office hours, but—oh, never mind. It's a bad idea."

"Jane, it's okay. Please go on."

She releases a breath. "You've got so much on your plate, and now with Claude still off, then going part-time when he returns, but...well...I hoped I could cut my hours back a bit. Maybe finish at lunchtime for a little while so I can spend as much time as possible with Mum."

Her bottom lip wobbles but she is trying so hard to keep an emotionless expression. I go over and take her hands. She gazes at me, her eyes a brilliant blue from her unshed tears.

"Of course." I kiss away a tear. "You do what you must. There is nothing you are needed for with the merger yet anyway."

She manages a wobbly smile, relief filling her eyes. "Thank you." She embraces me and I return it, feeling her pain.

If I can make anything easier for her, I will. Liv does not have much longer left. Jane needs this time with her.

Chapter 17

Jane

There's a constant ball of dread in my stomach.

Two weeks.

Two *long* weeks since that awesome day out. Two weeks of working mornings and taking the afternoon off. I'm at the hospital from one p.m. until around eight p.m. We always have dinner together, then Jacques and I go home and crash soon after. Each day is more emotionally exhausting than the last.

Mum's spirits are high but her body is failing. The blackouts are more frequent but controlled with medication. Her mobility is almost non-existent. When she does stand, she needs support. Dad and I take her for regular walks in the gardens to ensure she gets plenty of fresh air.

It's so hard watching her slowly die. Although it's not even that slow. According to the doctor, it's quick. Not that it helps at all. The hardest part is the waiting. I don't want her to die, but I don't want to watch her suffer. Some days I just want it to be over. Does that make me a terrible person?

How do other people survive this? Some go through it for years. I can't even begin to imagine that.

Rubbing my eyes, I check the time on my computer. Noon. Time to leave. After logging off, I send Jacques a message telling him I'll meet him at the hospital later. Before I put my phone away it buzzes in my hand. It's a text from Madame Sabine reminding me of my final dress fitting tomorrow after work. I reply to confirm I'll be there. If Mum's well enough, and if the doctor clears her, I might ask if she wants to come with me.

Pushing my chair in, I slip my phone away then place the strap of my handbag on my shoulder. After bidding my colleagues goodbye, I make my way to the door, taking my coat off the rack.

Despite the emotional turmoil of seeing Mum deteriorate day by day, I'm thankful I've had this time with her. Over the last couple of weeks, I've been able to push the resentment aside and focus on making new memories. The upside is my wedding planning is done. I'm not kidding. Even the invites have been sent. It's a relief and I'm glad she's been part of it.

But how the hell can I get married without her?

Huffing, I leave the office and don my coat. Surely there must be something I can do.

➤➤➤ ◄◄◄

An idea comes to me in the early hours of the morning when I can't sleep. That's happening a lot lately. Insomnia. I'm usually a great sleeper, but the stress is getting to me. I can't settle. Can't relax. The ball of dread in my gut isn't moving and I have a constant fluttering in my chest.

The moment I wake up, I send a message to Madame Sabine, telling her my plan and asking if she can help. It's very last minute but time is of the essence. A new feeling is settling in place...that Mum won't be around for much longer.

I push it aside for now, wanting to enjoy this afternoon with her. It might be our last.

By the time Jacques and I leave for work, with him driving, Madame Sabine replies saying she's available. Before I send a message back, I call the hospital. I must time it right because Doctor Wright is just clocking on, and I manage to speak to her. She promises to ring me back after visiting Mum.

"Everything okay?" Jacques asks while we're sitting in traffic.

I place my phone on my lap and nod, rubbing my chest. "Yeah, I'm planning a little surprise for Mum. I have my final dress fitting this afternoon and I want her to be there. I'm asking Madame Sabine if she can take some photos of us since..." I clear my throat and glance out the window, blinking away tears.

This is my plan. Have Mum see me in the whole outfit, have her done up nicely too, then Madame Sabine will take some photos. I'm hoping to coax Dad into coming along too.

Jacques' warm hand covers mine and he squeezes. "I think it's a great idea."

I draw in a breath and turn back to him, my bottom lip quivering. "Thanks. It's just...if she can't be there, I want some memory of her on our big day."

The traffic starts moving and he gives my hand one more squeeze before inching forward. Heaviness weighs on my shoulders. I was so excited to do this at two a.m. but now I'm just depressed. Because deep down, I'm aware this is my last chance to include Mum in anything wedding related.

This is supposed to be a new beginning with Jacques. Why is everything so final?

I mentally pull myself together when we arrive at the office, Jacques and I going our separate ways.

I'm an hour into my morning when Doctor Wright gets back to me, clearing Mum to go out on the proviso she sits as much as possible. If she must stand, she needs support.

I text Madame Sabine to tell her everything is sorted and ask if we can arrive a little bit earlier, so Mum can be back in time for dinner. She replies confirming this is fine and I breathe a sigh of relief.

⟫⟫⟫ ⟪⟪⟪

"Hi Mum, Hi Dad," I greet when I arrive at the hospital this afternoon.

Dad gives me a little wave but goes back to reading an English newspaper. His hair is neat and he's wearing dress trousers, a shirt, and a tie. There was no time to organise a suit. He's been sworn to secrecy, and I left him in charge with making sure he and Mum were ready on time.

It took a bit of encouragement to get him to join us, but he agreed in the end. This might just be our last chance to have a family photo together too.

My heart grows heavy. There are too many 'lasts' for my liking.

"Alright, what's going on?" Mum asks when I arrive, a glint in her eyes.

Thanks to the lovely nurses only too willing to help, her hair has been styled. She's also wearing a light coat of makeup and a pretty dress, but I've asked Madame Sabine to organise something in light blue.

"It's a surprise." I kiss her cheek. "Have you both had lunch?"

She nods, looking at me curiously. "Yes. Where are we going? Can you tell me that?"

"It's my final fitting today. Where are your shoes?"

Mum points to them in the corner near Dad. He overhears and hands them to me.

"I need to wear makeup for a dress fitting?" Mum asks.

"Yep." I help her with her shoes. "Now, are you both ready to go?"

"Wait, your father is coming?" Mum's brow is creased in confusion.

"Yes," I say with a laugh. "Why else is he dressed up too? Now stop asking questions and let's go."

Mum sighs but she's smiling. She's enjoying every second of this.

After a goodbye to some of the nurses, we leave. For a short while I can forget about my other worries and focus on the excitement. It's a beautiful day today too. It's still early spring but it's unseasonably warm and sunny.

The hospital has organised a taxi that can fit Mum's wheelchair and we make it to the bridal store in record time. By the time we're inside though, I'm emotional. The enormity of what today means hits me. Tears sting my eyes and a lump lodges itself in my throat. I can't lose control. I don't want to. I want to make happy memories.

I see Madame Sabine through the window, and she spots me at the same time. Her smile is bright and welcoming as she rushes over to the door. Instantly the emotion fades, and calmness washes over me. She's like that. So upbeat that you can't help but feel her vibes.

"*Salut*! Come in, come in!" She holds open the door and I push Mum through, Dad following.

"You may leave your lovely mother here, Jane," Madame Sabine instructs. "I will help her get ready while you change. Your dress is hanging in the dressing room. Monsieur Collins, you may take a seat here." She gestures to a plush long bench opposite the viewing platform.

Dad nods and sits on one end, looking relieved to be out of the way.

"Get me ready?" Mum asks.

I grin at her. "Just go along with it." I dash off to change.

The excitement is returning as I pull the curtains across and start to undress. I want to relish this moment and not think about what's looming over us.

Once I'm down to my underwear, I gaze at my dress and breathe out a shaky breath. Gosh it's beautiful.

Taking it off the hanger, I step into it. A young assistant, who doesn't speak or understand English, helps me into it then disappears. I turn to the mirror and stare. Oh yes. It fits like a glove and the alterations are perfect.

Grinning, I start tidying up my hair. I brought some ties and clips with me, so I style it into a half up-do. When that's done, I touch up my eyeliner and lip gloss, keeping makeup to a minimum, then smooth down my dress.

Pulling the curtains across, Madame Sabine comes over to fix up my train.

"You are *très beau*," she says, facing me. "Wait here *une minute*." She holds up a finger and rushes away.

Seconds later she returns with my veil and fits the comb into my hair.

"There!" She clasps her hands in front of her chest. "Turn around."

I do so, looking into the floor-to-ceiling mirror. My breath catches. I can't wait for Jacques to see me in this.

"Now, come." Madame Sabine takes my arm. "We must take some photos, *non*? I have someone special to help."

"What?"

Madame Sabine clicks her fingers. The assistant and another young woman holding a fancy camera appear.

"*Bonjour*," the photographer greets with a little bow of her head.

My mouth opens and closes a couple of times. "Madame Sabine, this is too much. I was going to use my phone."

"Oh *non, non, non*!" Her hand flies to her forehead. "This is a very upsetting time for you and your family, this is a little gift from *moi*."

"Thank you so much." I lean in and embrace her, a couple of tears escaping.

She pulls away and tuts. "Your tears are black." Shaking her head, she tells the assistant to grab some tissues. When she has them, she blots them away.

"Now, come, your parents are waiting."

I nod and she leads me back to the viewing area. Dad hasn't moved and Mum is out of her chair, sitting next to him. She's dressed in a stunning light blue and crème dress. They both look up when I enter. Dad's jaw drops but he pulls himself together, a proud smile stretching across his face. Mum promptly bursts into tears, the same way she did the first time we visited.

I rush over to sit beside her, and we embrace. "Surprise."

We pull apart and Mum is smiling, her eyes shimmering. "What's all this about?"

I go to speak but a lump forms in my throat. Swallowing over it, I say, "If you can't be there...at the wedding...I still want something I can look back on."

"Oh, Jane." She takes my hand and clasps it.

I wish so much this was different. I want her at my wedding, there must be something—

I gasp when it comes to me. "Wait, wait I have an idea!"

Madame Sabine and the assistant are whispering and moving around, setting up for photos, oblivious to our conversation. The photographer is flitting about snapping random pictures.

"We can bring it forward!"

I sit straighter in my seat, a surge of adrenalin rushing through my veins. Yes! Why didn't I think of this sooner? "Jane—"

"We can ask the celebrant to come to the hospital," I interrupt.

"Jane—"

"Or if you're up for it, we can find a registry office." I glance at her expectantly, my heart racing. "Don't you see? You don't have to miss it!"

This is a great idea! Jacques won't mind either. We can have a second wedding in The Maldives for other family and friends.

"Jane." Mum takes my face between her hands. "I need you to listen to me, okay?"

My excitement vanishes. A sob rises in my throat because I know what she's going to say.

"Mum," my voice breaks, "please don't do this."

"Jane, please, are you listening?"

Swallowing, I manage a nod, but tears are relentlessly sliding down my cheeks now.

"Please don't give up your dream for me."

"But—"

She moves her hands to take mine. "No but's. Jane, you're my daughter, my only child, and all I want is for you to be happy. I want you to have everything you've ever dreamed of."

"But what about *your* dreams?" My bottom lip quivers. "I want to make them come true. Why won't you let me?"

"Oh, Jane. My darling daughter." She embraces me and I breathe in her motherly scent, wanting to commit it to memory. "Don't you understand?"

We pull back and I sniffle, shaking my head.

"I *do* have everything." She strokes my cheek. "You're the daughter every mother dreams of. You've found the most wonderful man in Jack. I have my own amazing husband. I don't need anything else. I've got everything I ever wanted or needed. As much as I'd love to see you get married, seeing you now..." She shakes her head and scans me up and down. "I've got *more* than I ever dreamed of."

"Oh Mum." I fall into her arms and we embrace again.

"Wonderful!"

We pull apart and I turn around to see the photographer taking photos as Mum and I are talking.

"Oh, I'm a mess." I laugh weakly and wipe away tears that leave black streaks on my hands.

"*Non*," Madame Sabine says with a smile. "You are *superbe*. Now, let us wipe away those tears and get some formal photos of all of you together."

Chapter 18

Jacques

Resting my elbows on the table, I place my head in my hands. The boardroom at Entreprises DuPont is heavy with tension. On my right, Claude is updating Rémy on the merger process. Or more specifically, that we have stalled. On my left, Hayden is drumming his fingers on the table.

It is Friday, and earlier this week Rémy dug up some hidden records for Entreprises DuPont. Questionable contracts and financial statements that made no sense. Money coming in from people not on the client list. Money going out for expenses that, on paper, appear to have no business relevance.

The further we delve into the merger, the deeper we dig, and the more issues we find.

We sent the financial documents back to the accountant and the contracts to the lawyers. I always suspected Papa of conducting shady business but never had any evidence. Until now.

I have no idea how it will affect the merger, but it could ruin everything. If it ends up being too risky to merge with my company, I will be left to run both. This is what I have been trying to avoid because it will mean Jane and I cannot go back to Surfers Paradise. We will logistically not be able to.

Why did I think this was a good idea?

With a heavy sigh, I glance up and into the eyes of my brother sitting opposite me. He appears frozen in place. His hair is stuck up on end. Dark bags under his eyes. Pale face. He's contrite, though he does not need to be. This is not his fault.

I reach for my laptop and pull it forward. I stare at the screen, only seeing a wall of text. I cannot make out words. My brain feels as if it is stuffed with cotton wool.

It has been one month since Jane and her parents had their afternoon out and photoshoot. One more month trying to figure out this merger and hitting a brick wall. Rémy is not the only one showing signs of exhaustion. I am feeling it, and even Hayden is looking worse for wear. He must be eager to return home already.

"Jacques?"

I blink and turn to Claude who is looking at me expectantly. "Sorry." I shake my head. "What was the question?"

My phone buzzes on the table. It is face down so I cannot see who it is from.

"I didn't ask a question," he snipes. "I said that until we've heard back from the accountant and lawyers, we should just focus on business as usual."

Claude may be part-time and not feeling the pressure as much, but he certainly sounds as frustrated as the rest of us.

I nod. "Fine, business as usual it is. Rémy, contact someone from the IT department and ask them to dig deeper into the files. We need to make sure there are no other hidden surprises."

When he does not respond, I glance up at him. He has not moved. His expression is blank, eyes distant.

"Rémy," I repeat louder.

He blinks. "What was that?"

I am not the only one struggling to concentrate today. I repeat what I said.

He nods. "Yes, I will contact them after the meeting." He clears his throat and rakes a hand through his hair.

"Staff are getting antsy," Hayden speaks up. "We need to give them an update."

"I agree." Claude grabs his mouse and clicks on his screen a couple of times. "Let's write an email now. We promised transparency and over the last month we haven't done that. If we keep them in the dark too much longer, it may result in more resignations."

My phone buzzes again, but I ignore it.

"We cannot afford to have anymore," I say. "We have exhausted our backlist of possible candidates. Anyone else we hire will have to go through the hiring process and we do not have time for that."

We replaced five people from the ten resignations. It is better than nothing, but it will not be long before we feel the loss. Out of the list of previous applicants we had kept on record, most were employed or no longer interested.

"We use the resources we have," Hayden says matter-of-factly. "We all pull together, share the workload, and ask if anyone can work overtime." He nods at Claude whose fingers are hovering over the keyboard. "In the email, maybe put a call out for anyone willing to put in some extra hours."

Claude starts typing as he and Hayden continue discussing the wording.

My mobile vibrates with another message.

An idea comes to me, and thinking aloud, I say, "We should have a team building day."

Hayden and Claude stop talking and turn to me.

"The staff from company do not know each other. A team building day will bring everyone together."

"Great idea mate," Hayden says. "The weather is getting warmer, how about a day out?"

We throw about some ideas and Rémy starts pitching in too. It takes us another twenty minutes but once it's done, Claude sends it. During the discussion, my phone buzzes a few more times and I am getting worried. I have not been able to check it, but something tells me it is bad news. What if it is Liv?

In the last month, Liv's condition has deteriorated rapidly again. It was the day after the photoshoot when the doctor said she had little time left. Swept away on a whirlwind of emotion, Jane and I have become like ships passing in the night.

Every weekday consists of work, hospital, sleep. The weekends for me are work with hospital visits later in the afternoon. For Jane, she spends both days at the hospital. We have spent little time together, only to sleep, occasionally eat, but never to sit down and talk. There is no way I would ever stop her from seeing her dying mother, but I miss her closeness. Her happiness.

She rarely smiles nowadays. I understand how difficult this is for her and I am thankful we at least go to bed together. Every night I hold her close, tell her I love her, and promise her that I am here.

Because despite how crazy our lives are right now, she does not need to do this alone.

We conclude the meeting and stand. This is the final one for the day.

"I want everyone to have a proper weekend." I make sure to meet the gaze of all three of them. "No sneaking any work in." I direct my glare at Hayden.

He has been instrumental since his arrival, picking up what Claude cannot do and more, but I worry he is working too hard.

He grins and mock salutes but there is relief in his eyes.

I intend to spend the whole weekend with Jane. If that is at the hospital, I do not mind so long as we are together. Unfortunately, Liv is bedridden now and sleeps most of the time. When we visit, we sit and talk in the hopes that she can hear us being normal. Jane says this is what she would want.

I close my laptop and reach for my phone when there is a knock on the boardroom door. It bursts open and Rémy's young assistant enters, panting. She scans the room and rests her gaze on me.

My heart jumps to my throat and I hold my breath.

"Excuse me Monsieur DuPont, I have an urgent message from your fiancée. She said you are needed at the hospital immediately." She bows her head as she backs out of the room, closing the door after her.

Everyone in the room stares at me. I release the breath I'm holding.

An urgent message from your fiancée.

Nausea washes over me, my heart stuttering to a stop. I swallow the bile rising in my throat as I glance at the three other men in the room. My brother and two close friends. All whom I trust implicitly.

All wearing the same grim expression. The room begins to spin as a whirlwind of emotions and responsibilities fills my mind. I need to be there for Jane, but there is still so much to be done here.

My gaze shifts back to Rémy who has turned pale. He has spent a lot of time with Liv when he volunteers at the hospital. This cannot be easy on him either.

"Go," Claude urges without an ounce of hesitation.

His words do not sink in at first.

"Jacques," Claude repeats. "You must go. Now."

I blink a couple of times as I gain the ability to move again. I jump to my feet and glance around, debating what to do. I reach for my laptop, doing the one thing I can control—packing up and putting my things away.

"Jacques." It is Rémy this time.

I stop and look across at my brother.

"We will tidy up for you," he adds. "Leave everything, just take your phone."

"Do you want to come with me?" I ask.

He is startled for a second but shakes his head. "No, I think I will be more helpful here." He sits upright in his chair, appearing to grow before my eyes. Confident. Businesslike. It is as though he finally realises how important this is and he is ready to step up. "We can handle this," he adds, looking at Claude and Hayden who nod.

"Don't worry about anything mate," Hayden says. "Family always comes first."

When everyone agrees, this snaps me into action. Family. Yes, Liv is family.

"Thank you, all of you." I grab my phone and rush out of the office.

Once I'm on the street, I finally check the multiple messages, all from Jane begging me to hurry. I send her a message straight away.

I am on my way.

I only hope I am not too late.

Chapter 19

Jane

I end the call after leaving a message with reception. *Where is he?*

Tears sting my eyes for the umpteenth time as I also send him one last text, cursing the stupid merger and the stupid meetings.

Where are you? Mum is asking for you.

She has been sleeping more over the past month but had moments when she could talk, laugh, and be her jovial self. She's been eating less but would at least manage a few bites of every meal.

Over the past three days though, she's refused food, will only sip a little water, and slips in and out of consciousness. Today she's already woken twice to say she loves me and Dad. I know this is it. She's only waiting for one person. Jacques.

Another half an hour passes, the knot of anxiety grows in my stomach. I'm considering sending another message when my phone vibrates in my hand and my heart leaps. It's Jacques. At last.

I am on my way.

I breathe a sigh of relief and reach for Mum's hand, squeezing it. "He'll be here soon, Mum."

She doesn't respond, but a small smile forms on her lips. Her hand lightly squeezes mine. Two tears drip down my cheeks but I don't bother to wipe them away. They've been relentless.

I'm so glad I've had this extra time with her. As much as I don't want her to die, I'm at peace with the knowledge that I did all I could. I'm going to miss her like crazy, and the next few days, weeks, months, maybe even years, are going to be so hard. But I don't want her to suffer anymore. It's time for her to go.

My gaze lands on the table beside her bed where three framed photos sit. It's one of those triple frames that fold open and close. The one on the left is of Mum, Dad, Jacques, and me in front of the Eiffel Tower that was taken on our day out. The middle photo is of me, Mum, and Dad taken at the bridal store. The right one was also taken at the bridal store, and is of Mum and me looking at the camera with our arms around each other, grinning like the best of friends. And that describes her so well. Not just my mother, but my best friend.

I duplicated this one and sent a copy to Madame Sabine to say thank you. She didn't charge me any extra, even though she paid for a professional photographer. I offered again to contribute but she refused.

Many photos were taken in the last two months, and I have treasured copies of all of them.

After a few moments, I plant a kiss on Mum's hand and join Dad standing at the window, staring out. I loop my arm through his and rest my head on his shoulder.

"How are you, Dad?"

His body shudders as he silently cries. It's him I'm worried about most. I've got Jacques, and even though we've both been so busy, he's always been there at the end of the day to comfort me as we sleep. Without that, I might've fallen apart. I resent his job and the merger, but I understand he can't just stop. The timing is terrible, that's all.

I hold onto Dad's arm and we cry together.

"I don't want to lose her," he whispers, drawing in a shuddering breath. He's tried so hard to be strong for Mum but sometimes he loses control.

"I know, but you don't have to go through this alone. Jack and I are both here for you."

He nods and removes a tissue from his pocket to wipe his eyes and nose.

"I'll be right," he says, patting my arm.

I can see on his face that he *won't* be alright. He's got the typical Aussie 'she'll be right mate' attitude, but it's not doing him any good today. I'm not sure how we're going to help him with the merger still going on, but I need to figure something out. I can't let him go home alone and expect he'll be okay.

Mum groans. Dad and I turn to see her wincing and writhing. Her hands come up to her head and she cries out in pain. We've seen this a few times and it's always my undoing. Tears threatening, I tell Dad I'm going to find a nurse and rush out of the room. One of the middle-aged nurses happens to be coming in and we nearly collide.

"Oh, I'm s-sorry," I stammer through sobs.

The nurse stops and kindly slides her arm across my shoulders. "You don't have to be sorry dear. I'm going to go in and give your mother some more morphine."

I nod and run my hands down my face to rid the tears, but this only makes way for more. Any second now and I'm sure my heart is going to burst out of my chest. This was never meant to happen. Mum was supposed to live until she was ninety or older. A bloody brain tumour wasn't meant to claim her life.

I slide down the wall until I'm resting on my haunches with my back against it. I need a few moments. I've tried not to let Dad witness me cry. I'm trying to make it as easy for him as possible. Always smile, be happy. It must work as generally he's in positive spirits when we're together.

But I only have so much strength and there's very little left in reserves. Something will give sooner or later unless I can find a way to top them up. For Dad. I cradle my head and focus on breathing. I'm not sure how long I stay like this but eventually I pull myself together.

Lowering my hands, I glance up and down the hallway at the bustling nurses and wonder how they do this. Being in a palliative ward must be so stressful, having to witness death probably every day. I'm struggling with Mum. I don't think I could do it as a job. I give them so much kudos, they deserve it. They're true angels.

"Jane!"

I gasp and whip my head around to see Jacques running towards me. I leap to my feet and meet him halfway, flinging my arms around his neck. My tears come freely, yet again, but I don't care. He's here, and that's all that matters.

"Please tell me I'm not too late," he says when we pull apart, his face pale and his eyes full of fear.

I use a hand to wipe my tears away and shake my head. "You're not too late, but she's asking for you."

He visibly swallows and nods. I move away and take his hand as we go into her room together. Dad glances up when we enter, relief evident on his face when he spots Jacques.

"I'm glad you're here mate." Dad's voice is resigned. "She's been waiting for you."

I have never seen so much fear on Jacques' face as I do now. He squeezes my hand then lets it go and sits on the chair beside the bed. Taking Mum's hand between his own two large ones, the first thing he looks at is the photos on the bedside cupboard.

I gasp and my hand flies to my mouth. *Damn it.*

Usually, I hide it before he arrives, but today it completely slipped my mind. I'm not superstitious, I never thought it would bring bad luck for him to see me in my wedding dress, but I *did* want to surprise him. I want to witness his expression on the day I walk down the aisle.

But when he turns back to me, his smile lighting up the room, I realise this is enough. My heart flutters and a little bit of tension dissipates. I glance at Mum who is awake, watching the exchange with a full-on smile. How can I be annoyed? I can't, and I'm not. It's perfect.

"Isn't she beautiful?" Mum whispers.

Jacques looks at Mum, the photo, then back at her. "Yes, she is." He glances back at me again, his eyes shining. "*Si beau.*"

"Take care of her Jack." Mum's voice grows weak. "Please take care of my girl."

He breaks down and holds her hand to his cheek. My heart pounds uncomfortably in my chest but I'm too frozen to move.

"*Je promets*," he says. In English he repeats it, "I promise." In a whisper, he adds in French, "*Je t'aime Maman*."

No translation is needed. Her bright smile when she lets go of his hand and reaches out to caress his cheek, telling him she loves him too, is evidence that she understands. Mum looks at Jacques, me, and finally Dad.

"I love you all, my family," are her final words as she closes her eyes and takes her last breath.

I hear a strangled cry and it's only as I fall to my knees in a flood of tears that I realise it came from me. Jacques wastes no time coming over, sitting beside me, and wrapping me in his embrace as we both sob. I watch through tear-filled eyes as Dad stares in shock at his beloved wife lying motionless on the bed.

"Liv?" His voice breaks. "Liv?" He goes over and shakes Mum's shoulder. "C'mon love, this isn't funny."

"Dad," I call out, my voice hoarse. "Dad, she's gone."

It's like a bomb going off in the distance. Silence at first. He glances over at me, his expression blank. The pieces appear to come together as he notices me and Jacques on the floor crying. He glances back at Mum, his mouth opening and closing wordlessly.

The shock hits and Dad's sobs come out in loud broken cries as he shakes Mum's shoulder a little harder. "Liv? Liv? You're not allowed to do this. You promised you wouldn't go before me."

His sobs break my heart and I close my eyes to the image of my father standing heartbroken over his wife's body. I bury myself in Jacques' warm embrace, wondering when the crying will stop. Wondering if the pain will ever go away. Maybe it won't? Most of all I'm wondering how the hell I'm going to leave Dad alone.

When I open my eyes again, I'm left with the haunting image of nurses coming in and out of the room, Dad lying next to Mum, holding her one last time, sobbing and begging her to come back. He's not my father right now. He's a lost man who has no idea how to navigate this new life.

It's now that I make the hardest decision of my life.

I must go back to Australia with Dad.

I have no idea what that means about anything else, but I can't even think about that. Dad can't go back alone. I'm his only family and he needs me.

Chapter 20

Jacques

The last time I experienced this type of grief was when Aimée left when I was a boy, but I was forced to bury it.

When Papa passed away, I mourned the loss of the father he could not be, but there was no sorrow or heartbreak. Only relief that he could do no more damage to my family, or anyone else.

Liv's passing is so different. I am allowed to grieve, no one is forcing me to bury it, but the pain that comes with it is unbearable.

There is an emptiness within me that I am unsure how to fill. Not even Jane can fix it. These are emotions I am unfamiliar with. I remember experiencing a similar darkness last year when we were separated, but this is different. Deeper. It has been one week since she died, and I am unsure how to move past it.

Jane and I are grieving in our own way...but not together. We live in the same apartment, share the same bed, but the closeness and intimacy are gone.

Yet we have received support from people who barely knew Liv. Claude and Penny visited with Amélie and Henri, always with food in hand. So did Aimée, Tavish, and Avril. We have so much in the freezer, I have not had to cook for the whole week. Even coworkers and neighbours have sent condolences.

The last week passed by in a blur. I returned to work while Jane took the week off. We have remained like ships passing in the night. In an attempt to deal with the grief, I am burying myself in work. It is the only thing I can do. Otherwise, it is like there is an invisible wall shutting me off.

Jane has spent every moment with William. Helping him through his extreme grief. He is in a bad way and spends most days in the spare room. Hayden went to stay with Rémy after Liv passed.

It is now Friday evening and I arrive home to find Jane and William sitting at the kitchen table. A piece of paper and a pen is in front of her. It appears to be a checklist.

"*Bonsoir,*" I greet, closing the door behind me.

"Insurance is sorted." Jane ticks the paper. "Cremation was today." She glances up at me and utters a brief, "Hi," and continues with, "You were going to come with me tomorrow, right Dad?"

William is staring off into space, his eyes cloudy.

"Dad." Jane pokes his arm with her pen.

"Huh?" William blinks and turns to her.

"You said you were going to come with me to pick up the ashes tomorrow." Jane's tone holds a hint of frustration.

He rakes a hand over his head and down his face. "I'd rather not." He gets to his feet and when he spots me, his smile is tight. "Good day, Jack?"

I witness the frustration on Jane's face before she covers it with her hands.

The air is tense and I feel awkward in my own apartment. I stand in front of the door, waiting for Jane to run up and greet me the way she used to, but it never comes.

"It was fine, thank you," I say.

William nods and shuffles from foot to foot. "Righto. I'm going to rest before dinner."

He pauses, glances from me to Jane then walks away.

I gaze at Jane but she won't make eye contact. I do not understand how Liv's death has put such a chasm between us. The day she died, I never felt closer to Jane. We held each other, crying together, and I was certain we would work through this. But now, I have never felt so far apart, even when we were separated by countries.

"Jane," I say and she looks up. "I will come with you tomorrow. When you pick up the ashes."

She stares at me unblinking. "You will? Why?"

Does she even need to ask? "To support you, why else?"

"Thanks, but don't worry about it. I can manage."

"I never said you cannot, but you should not have to do this alone."

She gets to her feet, glaring at me. "Why bother? I've been doing everything else on my own while you've been working." She steps out from the chair and pushes it in.

Her words hit me hard, crushing my heart. That was low.

"I have offered," I defend, keeping my tone even. "Every day I ask if I can help. You always say you are fine. I asked if you wanted me to take time off work and you said no." I go around to her and take her hands. "You're shutting me out Jane, but I want to help you."

Her bottom lip wobbles and she groans, rubbing her eyes. "I'm sorry," she mumbles, her face crumbling.

"We should be supporting each other right now." I gather her in my arms and hold her close.

It is the first time in nearly a week that she has let me hold her.

"But...the merger. You have so much to do," she says against my chest, her voice muffled.

I sigh and tighten my embrace around her. "I have three other men who are doing a great job when I am not there."

She does not need to know that it is still moving at a snail's pace. Not now, at least.

The accountant came back with her report, giving us the all-clear. Although she recommends getting the police involved for the missing funds, which are in an offshore account. Before I do anything, I will wait to hear from the lawyers.

I blink and bring myself back to the present. I should be worrying about Jane, not thinking about work.

"Okay," she says, stepping out of my embrace.

"Okay?"

She nods. "I'd like you to come with me tomorrow. It's our last chance to say g-goodbye." A couple of tears drip down her cheeks.

"Then I will be there."

Maybe this will be the turning point for us.

Picking up the ashes is a straight-forward process even if receiving them is emotional. I am uplifted somehow. Like a fog lifted and I can see clearly. Closure I think people call it. A door is opening, and I can finally escape the darkness.

Although it appears to have the opposite effect on Jane. When we leave, she is holding a box with the ashes in it, her shoulders slouched.

"It's surprisingly heavy," she says with a small smile.

"Would you like me to take it?"

She shakes her head and holds it closer to herself. "No, it's okay."

Our walk to the car is in silence and it continues on our way home.

When I stop at a red light, Jane says in a soft voice, "I'm going back to Australia with Dad."

The light turns green, but I do not move. My heart sinks as I turn to her. She's staring straight ahead. There has been no hint of this, but it must have been on her mind for a while. Why did she not talk to me?

A horn beeps behind me, and I avert my attention back to the road. The light is still green, so I put my foot down and speed forward. Drawing in a deep breath, I flex my fingers on the steering wheel, trying to come to terms with the news.

"Can we talk about it?" I ask calmly, glancing at her but she is still staring ahead.

"We're planning to fly out tomorrow." She clears her throat and folds her hands in her lap. "I wanted to be sure there were no hold-ups today, so I'll book the flights once I'm home. Dad really needs some normalcy, it'll help him recover."

Panic builds in my chest. I draw in a calming breath before speaking again. "You did not mention anything about going back to Australia."

She will not look at me. Her lips purse into a thin line when I glance over at her.

"It's pretty obvious, Jacques."

My heart stutters to a stop. *Jacques.*

The atmosphere in the car turns frigid. Jane turns to me, horror written across her features. It should not be a big deal, it is just a name, but she has addressed me as Jack from the first day we met. Apart from one or two occasions, or if she is introducing me to someone.

Turning down the next side street, I pull over abruptly and turn to her. She meets my gaze and there is a storm of withheld emotions in her eyes. My shock peters out and I let it go. A lot is going on and this should not be a big deal.

"I'm sorry," she whispers, her bottom lip quivering. She covers her face with her hands. Her shoulders start shaking as she sobs silently.

It is awkward in the car, but I manage to hold her close as she cries.

After a few moments, she pulls away and faces me. "Dad doesn't see it right now, but he needs me. He needs support. Yeah, he's got mates at home but he's going back to the house he shared with Mum. I can't let him do that alone."

I swallow but nod. She has a point and there is no way I will stop her, but I will not let her throw away our relationship too. We have been through too much and come too far to let something like this break us.

"I will come with you," I say matter-of-factly.

"No, Jack, I don't want you to."

I don't want you to.

Those five words slap me in the face so hard I jerk away. She is not looking at me again and my world falls out from beneath my feet.

She shakes her head and mutters something before huffing out a breath. "I didn't mean it like that," she backpedals. "I just...I don't want you dropping everything for me. *Again.*"

I stare at her. "Jane, when will you understand that I will *always* drop everything for you?"

She worries her bottom lip with her teeth, eyebrows drawing together. "You're needed here. Besides, I think I need this. I need to do it for Dad. For me, even. Maybe it'll help me heal too."

I slouch in my seat. How can I argue with that?

"What about us?" I hold my breath in anticipation. "Our future? Your job? We have so much planned."

Her eyes are sad. "I don't know, Jack. I don't know anything anymore."

And just like that, everything I thought I knew is so uncertain. The woman of my dreams is slipping away. The wedding. Everything.

I thought going with Jane to pick up the ashes was a turning point, and it was.

In the wrong direction.

Chapter 21

Jane

I don't know what to do anymore.

I'm so lost. So empty. I'd hoped picking up the ashes would help with closure. It only widened the gaping hole in my heart.

The drive is in silence. I've hurt Jacques. His knuckles are white as he grips the steering wheel. I hate that I'm doing this, but what else can I do? The last thing I want is to lose what we have, but I can't stop my actions. I'm like a spring bouncing around out of control.

The chasm between us is completely my fault.

When we arrive home and he parks the car, we sit in silence a little longer. I don't remember there ever being this much silence between us.

Ugh.

He turns to me, his eyes dark and stormy. "Are you sure you need to do this?"

"Yes," is all I manage. I'm incapable of thinking about anything else.

For the last week, I've been running on adrenalin. I can't believe I accused him yesterday of not helping. Of course he's offered. Every single day. I always said no. Only because I didn't know how he could help. There was literally nothing he could do. But I didn't have to shut him out. He could've helped just by being there. I didn't let him.

Grief is a weird thing, I realise. It affects everyone so differently.

Jacques buried himself in work. More than normal.

Dad hasn't done much at all. He spends his days sitting and staring at the wall. No jogging. No walks. No going anywhere at all. Just drowning in his grief.

Me? Well, I guess I'm like Jacques. I'm a doer, I keep busy, which means I haven't stopped. I haven't even grieved. That's why I'm hitting an invisible wall now and shutting Jacques out. I'm not even doing it intentionally. It is some kind of instinctive protective measure.

"Okay," he says, filling the silence. "But please don't give up on us."

I gaze into his imploring eyes, but even though I know what I *should* say, the words die on my tongue.

Instead, I slip out of the car and go upstairs to the apartment.

I have flights to book.

>>>> <<<<

I managed to book flights for this afternoon, Sunday. We'll fly back to the Gold Coast first, so I can see Bella and pick up Moe, then return to Adelaide the next day.

This morning Jacques and I are getting ready like it's any other. All that's different is the direction we're going. Jacques to the office for a few hours and I'm flying back to Australia. By the time he gets home, I'll be gone with no idea of what our future will entail.

Heaviness settles in the pit of my stomach.

When he kisses my cheek goodbye, lingering for a few seconds, everything still feels normal. Until he sighs and pauses as though he wants to say something. He's so close I can feel his warmth. Breathe in his familiar scent. But I don't dare look at him for fear of breaking down.

Another sigh then he turns.

"I'm lost," I blurt, knowing I need to say something. Anything. "I'm not coping, Jack. I need to go back home."

My heart is racing but I keep my gaze averted.

"Is this not your home?" he asks.

In my periphery, I watch him step closer to me again. Bottom lip quivering, I turn to him. "It's not the same. I need to be close to Mum. Please try to understand."

He stares at me for a long moment, nodding. "I understand," he whispers, before turning and leaving.

When the door clicks shut seconds later, the enormity of the situation hits me hard.

I gasp and spin around, staring at the closed door. I should go after him. I should ask him to drop everything, like he said he would, and come back with me.

But my feet are frozen in place.

By the time I pull myself together, too much time has passed, and he's gone. I could go after him, but I don't have the strength. My racing heart breaks in two and with trembling hands, I grab my phone and send a group chat to Penny and Avril.

Are you both free for an impromptu breakfast? I have news.

I need to act like everything is normal. Besides they'll never forgive me if I leave without seeing them. They deserve to know what's going on. Just not all the sordid details.

Dad comes out of his room and grunts a good morning. He doesn't appear overly chirpy, which is nothing out of the ordinary over the past week, but I thought he'd be happy to go home.

Maybe he's overwhelmed? I wouldn't blame him.

"Jack's gone to the office," I tell him. "I'll book an Uber to take us to the airport later. Can you be ready by four?"

Dad grunts again. "I guess so."

I hesitate, contemplating whether to ask what's wrong but decide against it. I don't want to smother him or question his grief.

"I need to go out this morning," I add. "Will you be okay? You're welcome to come if you want."

Dad places a mug under the nozzle of the coffee machine. "I'll be fine, Jane."

I look at him hard and sigh. Hopefully once he's home and able to settle again he'll start to recover. Him going home, and me going with him, *must* be the right thing. Otherwise, I'm giving up everything for nothing.

"Alright, I'll catch you in a couple of hours." I plant a kiss on his cheek then leave, dismissing the uncomfortable sensation in the pit of my stomach.

What if this is wrong? What if Dad doesn't want to go back? I haven't talked to him about it.

Scrap that. I haven't talked to him about anything *at all*. I've just assumed it's for the best. I shouldn't be so presumptuous, but I don't want to overwhelm him. It feels right but maybe...maybe I should ask what he wants.

Too late now, isn't it?

I wince as I step out onto the street, the warm spring sun kissing my skin.

By the time I arrive at the café, the girls have replied saying they'll be there. Penny is on her way and Avril says she will be half an hour. Penny must be closer because she arrives at the same time I do. When she spots me, she lights up and waves me over. It feels like a lifetime since I've seen her. Yes, she and Claude visited with the kids over the last week, but we never got to talk. The kids needed their attention, so it was a 'hi-bye' visit as they dropped off some food.

Either way, she's positively *glowing*.

I run up to her and we embrace. Gosh it's great to see her. We've been going through our own problems and couldn't be there for each other, but it hasn't come between us as friends.

We pull apart and grin at each other.

"I've missed you," we say at the same time and laugh.

"You look amazing, Pen." I step back and take her in from head to toe. I hadn't heard from her or Claude about their decision on the baby. But as I take her in and spot a small protrusion through her shirt, I gasp.

"Yes, we're keeping the baby," Penny says, smiling widely.

"Oh my gosh, that's so great, Penny!" I turn serious then ask, "How are you though? Honestly?"

"I'm great," she says. "Really great. I mean, I still have a little way to go until I'm one hundred percent but having Claude around more has been such a godsend. I was so confused about the baby, but we've talked about it openly, considered all options, and even saw a therapist. It really helped, and I know keeping it is the right choice. But this will be our last, no doubt about it."

"I'm so happy for you." I link my arm through hers and gesture to the cafe. "Shall we go inside?"

It's come over cloudy during the short walk and a few spits of rain sting my cheeks.

Penny nods and we go in, sitting at a table by the window.

"Do you want a drink while we wait for Avril? My shout."

"Yes please, but I'm sticking to herbal tea now." She rubs her belly affectionately, a smile spreading across her face.

An unfamiliar pang of...*something*...makes my heart skip. Suddenly breathless and eyes stinging with unexpected tears, I avert my gaze to the menu board.

What's that all about?

"Look at you and that pregnancy glow," I say, trying to keep my voice even. "Now before you rub that baby out of you, tell me what tea you want?"

Penny chuckles and tells me her choice.

On the way to the counter, it occurs to me.

Jealousy.

It's so unlike me. I try so hard not to be a jealous person, but right now I want what Penny has.

With Jacques.

But is it even possible? I'm still so confused about everything.

I shake the thoughts out of my head and place my order with the barista. By the time I arrive back at the table and sit, I've composed myself. On top of everything else, I'm *not* going to let this bother me. It's the last thing I need to worry about.

Penny reaches over and grabs my hand, holding it tight.

"What's wrong?" I ask.

"Jane, I'm so sorry about your Mum. I've been a crappy friend through this whole ordeal."

"No, you haven't—"

She squeezes my hand, her eyes cloudy. "You don't have to be nice about it. I could've texted you more or called you. But—"

"Penny," I curl my fingers around hers, "you've had your own worries. It's okay, really. Besides, you and Claude brought around meals *every single day*. Like, how's that nothing? Okay so you didn't text every second of the day, but if you had I probably would've slapped you."

She laughs and relaxes, removing her hand and sitting back in her chair.

"Besides, I wasn't there for you either." I lower my face, guilt eating away at my insides. Deciding to go for total honesty, I add, "Even before Mum got really sick, I didn't know what to do. I didn't know if I *should* text. I had no idea how to deal with it and I'm sorry."

"Oh Jane, don't do that."

I blink and glance up, relieved that she's smiling.

"You know what? I didn't even notice, and I think leaving me and Claude to deal with it on our own was what we needed, so please don't feel bad."

I nod as my coffee, and Penny's tea are delivered.

"So," Penny leans forward, "what's the news? Are you pregnant too?" Her eyes light up. "Wouldn't that be amazing? Our kids could grow up together and—"

That stab is back but this time my stomach lurches. I stop her quickly. "Penny, no, I'm not pregnant." I force a laugh, but it hurts because she couldn't be further from the truth. "Besides, I won't confirm or deny anything. I want to wait until Avril arrives."

She appears disappointed and stares at me with her lips pursed.

I recognise the moment something twigs because she gets that familiar knowing expression on her face. "You're doing it again, aren't you?" she asks, folding her arms.

"What?" I avoid her gaze, running my finger over the top of my mug, the chocolate powder sticking to it.

"Running."

I lick the chocolate off then wipe my finger on a napkin. "I told you, I'm not confirming or denying anything until Avril is here. But I can say I'm not running."

Why does it feel like a lie?

Penny doesn't appear convinced, but she shrugs and sips her tea.

Her assumption plays on my mind, making me unsettled. She's given me something to think about at least. I'll have plenty of thinking time on the flight home, and when I'm back with Dad. He's not very talkative nowadays, it'll be a quiet existence.

My thoughts are interrupted by Avril breezing in and greeting us in her usual exuberant manner. I offer to shout her a coffee too and place another order. I also grab another for me and a top-up of tea for Penny.

Once I'm sitting again, Avril crosses one leg over the other, eyeing me critically. "Are you pregnant?"

Penny snorts a laugh and I glare at them both, throwing my arms up in exasperation. "Why does everyone think I'm pregnant all of a sudden?"

"You said you've got news," Avril says with a 'duh' expression. "Usually 'news' is code for pregnancy, engagement, or—" her eyes widen, and her mouth forms a perfect O. "Bad news. If you're breaking up with my brother, I swear—"

"We're not breaking up!" I say a little too loudly, and a few people glance over at us.

"I think she's running," Penny says. "She says she's not."

"Because I'm *not*. Ugh." I groan in frustration. "Will you hear me out? Please?"

Penny and Avril are sitting with their legs crossed and arms folded. It would be comical if I didn't feel like I was under interrogation.

"I'm going back to Australia," I blurt.

"Ha! I knew it!" Avril said pointing.

I rub my temples and sigh. "Avril, I didn't say we were breaking up, I said I'm going back to Australia. If you'd let me finish, I was going to add it's only for a little while to help Dad. He's in a bad place right now and I can't let him go back home alone."

Guilty expressions pass across the girls' faces and sad silence fills the air. Our drinks are delivered to the table, but they remain untouched.

"Sorry," Avril says, rubbing her nose. "I wasn't thinking."

"I'm sorry too," Penny says with a grimace.

I release a slow breath. When I'm in control I add, "Jack and I are fine, the wedding is going ahead, but we need to get over this. It's hit us all a lot harder than we anticipated. I can't leave Dad alone right now, and Jack must be here for the merger."

As the girls nod in understanding and come around to form a group hug, I wonder why I don't believe my own words.

Chapter 22

Jane

The warm Queensland sun beats down on me and I welcome it. Sitting outside the café I used to go to when Jacques and I lived here, I'm enjoying being back. I miss Jacques, of course, but there's something soothing about being here.

Dad and I arrived last night. After a long sleep, we woke up mid-morning. Dad is spending the day relaxing and I'm out to meet Bella so I can pick up Moe. She brought him to the clinic with her. We agreed to meet for a coffee and a chat first.

I've missed her. I've missed Moe.

But most of all, I miss Jacques.

We've been texting, but things are...weird. It doesn't help that neither of us are coming forward to talk. Or more specifically, *I'm* not talking and I'm giving off standoffish vibes so he can't. How do I stop it? Believe it or not, I so badly want to talk, clear the air, fix our relationship that is crumbling around our feet, but I can't. It's like some invisible force is stopping me.

Instead, I'm doing exactly what Penny said.

Running.

I can't deny the truth anymore and I'm using the excuse that Dad needs help to get through his grief. He does, that's not a lie, but I don't have to put Jacques' and my relationship on the line.

How do I break through that invisible wall? I wish someone would show me.

Being back in Queensland reminds me how much I love it here. How much I want this to be our home. It has been for nearly a year, and we've settled so well, but now it's slipping away. Since the merger began and Mum died, nothing is certain anymore.

We were meant to fly back here weeks ago but one thing led to another and we're still in Paris. Jacques and I haven't even spoken about our return. And the strangest thing? I don't mind. All I want is some certainty. Somewhere to put down roots. At this precise moment though, it seems like an impossible task.

"Jane?" a voice, not Bella's, calls. "Jane, is that you?"

I turn to the voice, my jaw dropping. "Regina?" I squeak. She's the last person I expect to see. We worked together on and off over the last couple of years, but last year we parted on bad terms and haven't spoken since.

She looks *so* different. Her hair is shorter, shoulder length, and dyed dark brown. In place of her oversized outfits are skin tight clothes. Denim shorts and a fitted white tank top that shows off her cleavage.

"Wow, it's so good to see you!" Regina says, stepping closer.

I remain seated so she's standing over me, the atmosphere growing awkward. We didn't part well last year and we haven't spoken or texted since. It feels rude not to greet her, so I stand and we hug awkwardly. I pull away quickly and sit.

"What are you doing here?" she asks. "I haven't seen you around for ages. I thought you'd gone back to Paris."

"Uh, we still have the apartment here but yeah, I was in Paris for a few weeks. Jack is merging his company with his father's, so he's been busy with that. I'm only back in Queensland for a couple of days..." I bite my tongue. Regina doesn't need the specifics of my personal life.

This would normally be the point where she'd raise an inquisitive eyebrow and try to push for more information. I wait for it, but it doesn't come. Regina hovers, shuffling from foot to foot, but she doesn't pry.

"How about a coffee?" she asks, gesturing to the empty seat.

"Oh, I'm meeting someone—"

"Jane!" Bella calls as if on cue and I see her running up behind Regina, waving.

I wave back. "Sorry, Regina I'll just be a moment." I jump to my feet, meeting Bella halfway for a long embrace. Such a different greeting to Regina's only moments earlier.

"It's so great to see you!" I exclaim when we pull apart.

"I'm sorry about your Mum." Her eyes are sympathetic and I know she understands. She lost her father a few years ago.

"Thanks, but I'm doing okay."

Sort of.

"I've saved us a table." I lead her to where Regina is standing. "Uh Bella, this is Regina. We used to work together."

Bella's eyes widen in realisation. She knows how things went down last year. "Hi, nice to meet you." She's friendly but curt.

"Uh, Jane have you got a tic?" Regina asks. "I don't want to interrupt. It'll only take a moment."

Bella waves me off. "It's fine. I'll shout you a coffee, the usual?"

I nod. "Yes thanks."

Regina and I move a few metres away from the table out of earshot, but closer to the beach.

When we stop on the edge of the path, Regina turns to me and runs an agitated hand through her hair. "Look, it's been a while, but I owe you an apology. For everything that happened last year." She looks me in the eye. "I was in a bad place and I took it out on everyone rather than addressing it. I'm sorry, Jane."

I nod. Not only was I not expecting to see Regina today, I also wasn't expecting an apology. I'd long forgotten about it.

"Apology accepted," I say with a smile. "We were both going through stuff at the time. But I hope things are better for you now?"

She nods without hesitation. "Much. I've changed jobs and embraced life." She glances across the beach and waves. "I should go, I'm meeting Vince and we're going surfing."

My eyebrows raise. "Vince the surfie hottie? He didn't do long term, right?"

She chuckles. "The one and only. After you and I parted ways, I went on a journey of self-discovery. I took up surfing lessons with him, we hit it off so well and he realised he just hadn't found the right woman to stay with long term." She grins and waggles her fingers on her left hand in my face. "We're getting married next year."

I gasp and embrace her properly this time. "Regina, that's amazing. I'm so happy for you."

"What about you and Jacques?" she asks, looking at my left hand then back at me with a grin. "Great ring choice. When's the big day."

"End of the year in The Maldives."

She rolls her eyes but it's not in spite. "Of course it is." She turns serious. "I am happy for you Jane. You were right, I was jealous and it was a bad look. I was a bit lost, but I've found myself now."

"I'm glad." I take a step back. "I should get back to Bella. Have a great life, Regina. I mean that."

Because even though we don't say the words, it's clear we're not meant to be friends. We're too different.

"Yeah, you too, Jane."

We embrace once more and we go our separate ways. When I sit down with Bella, I realise I have the people I need in my life. I don't have to be friends with everyone and that's okay. It may be the end of a friendship, but I'm starting a new chapter of my life.

⇢⇢⇢ ⇠⇠⇠

S tanding on the doorstep of my childhood home, the cat cage moves beneath my hand as Moe shuffles about, meowing impatiently.

We're back in Adelaide.

Dad is frozen in front of the door, holding his keys but not moving to unlock it. I can only imagine how difficult this is for him and it's taking all my willpower not to hurry him along. It's been a while since I've been back, but he's spent nearly every day here since he and Mum got married.

Moe's loud, mournful meow jerks Dad into action and he puts the key into the lock. I wait with bated breath as he turns it and the door swings open. The familiar scent of vanilla and flowers rushes out, along with a hint of mustiness from being closed up for too long.

My heart breaks all over again as memories of Mum, and my happy childhood in this home, come rushing out. Dad's sigh is all I hear as he forces himself inside. I can tell his legs are heavy by the way he moves so slowly and the thump of his shoes on the floorboards. Once we're in the hallway, Dad shuts and locks the door. We stand staring down to the other end of the house, which is the kitchen.

"Home sweet home," he says, bitterness lacing his tone.

I glance around at the familiar surroundings. Nothing has changed. The same happy family photos hang on the walls. The same furniture still in place. The only thing missing is Mum.

"I'm going to have a lay down," Dad says, turning to me. "I'm buggered."

I chuckle lightly and embrace him. "Sure thing. I might put Moe in the laundry for now to help him settle."

He nods. "I appreciate what you're doing Jane. Means a lot to me." His voice breaks and he blinks a couple of times. "I'm still not sure how I'm going to move on from this."

I reach for his hand. "That's why we're doing it together. Now you rest. How about I bring you in a coffee or something, once I've got Moe sorted?"

"Or something," he adds with a crooked smile. "Maybe a tea?"

"A tea it is."

He pats my hand. "You're a good girl, Jane." He disappears into his room, shutting the door after him.

I sigh and move my heavy legs towards the kitchen. The rest of our things are still in the car, which Dad kept at the airport long-term parking. I'll grab them later. In the kitchen, I empty the kettle and put it back on the boil with fresh water. While it's heating up, I go into the laundry and release Moe. The moment I open the cage door he dashes out with a loud meow, his tail fluffed. He stops near the washing machine, glaring at me.

He's fully grown now but still has his little moustache. When I picked him up from the vet, he was all over me. It was nice to be missed. Right now though, he's resenting me for keeping him confined and on a flight for a few hours.

"With that attitude, you can stay here and think about your actions," I say as I stand and pick up the cage.

When Moe hisses and swipes the air, I hiss back.

Gosh, what is the world coming to?

I go back out to the kitchen and shut the laundry door behind me. I'll keep Moe inside for a few days before letting him out so he can become familiar with his surroundings. The kettle clicks off and I steep a couple of teabags in two mugs. While they're brewing, I go searching for some snacks. Finding a packet of unopened Tim Tams, I put two on each saucer.

When the tea is ready, I go to Dad's room and knock. When he doesn't answer, I open the door and poke my head in. He's sitting on the edge of the bed again, holding Mum's pillow and sobbing into it. I place the mug down on his bedside cupboard then sit beside him, looping my arm through his and resting my head on his shoulder.

Time. That's the only healer right now.

Chapter 23

Jacques

The apartment is quiet without Jane or William. I especially miss Jane. She messaged when they arrived in Adelaide a few days ago, after picking up Moe from the Gold Coast, but her texts have been sporadic since. She told me being back home was hard and she needed some time. That she was not ignoring me.

Why does it feel like she is doing exactly that?

It has been one week and I have no idea what is going on or how she and William are doing. She must know I will worry about her. She should not have to deal with this alone, but she will not let me help her.

Did I not do something similar last year after Papa died?

She may not want to talk to me right now, but I do not want her to think I do not want to talk to her. I care and I want to help her, so I send a message.

You are not alone, *mon amour*. I am here. Always. *Je t'aime*.

I then send William a separate text.

If you need to talk, I am only a message away.

He has never been much of a texter, but I hope it will cheer him up.

There is a knock at my office door and Claude pokes his head in. "Jacques, we're supposed to have an online meeting with the lawyer and accountant. Rémy's joining us online and Hayden and I have set up in the boardroom."

"*Merde.* I forgot, sorry. I will be right there." As I stand, I ask, "Are there any hassles with the staff juggling Jane's workload?"

She has taken some time off as bereavement leave, but will work remotely when she is ready to return. Until then, her work is being divided amongst the staff.

Claude nods. "So far, so good." He stares at me hard, then asks. "Are you okay?"

"I will be if we can move forwards with the merger after today."

"Amen to that," he says as we exit my office. "Have you heard from Jane? Or William?"

I purse my lips and shake my head. "Not yet."

"I'm sure they're just busy."

I grunt a response but say nothing.

Am I really going to let Jane deal with this alone? Am I really going to let our relationship fizzle out?

Before I can think about this, we enter the boardroom and I close the door after me. I greet Hayden then sit and say into the camera, "Apologies for my lateness."

The meeting commences but my mind is everywhere except for where it should be. It is taking every ounce of willpower to remain focused. The lawyer is talking about loopholes and ways around the issue without bringing in the police or going to court. This is the ideal scenario and it helps me regain focus.

He and the accountant have been working together and have spoken to the companies affected and have come to an agreement. They will come to a fair settlement outside of court to pay out those who were wrongfully treated. The money found in offshore accounts was money stolen from these companies, which will be returned and a settlement paid on top.

Since everything happened under Papa's management and he is no longer alive, no police involvement is required. There has been no movement between the accounts, or new money added since Rémy moved into the role.

While I am past the stage of doubting my brother, there is still a sense of relief at hearing these words.

We will be able to move forwards with the merger again once these have been settled. The lawyer says in a week it should be sorted.

When the call ends, Hayden, Claude, and I release a collective sigh of relief.

"I think this calls for a celebration," Claude says. "How about lunch and a couple of drinks?"

Hayden agrees but I hesitate when I receive a message from William.

Thanks mate. Then we need to talk about Jane.

My breath catches and I am about to send a reply when another message comes through, this one from Maman. The last time I messaged her to ask if we could have coffee, she did not reply. Weeks have passed and this is the first I have heard from her.

I would like to see you now.

"Jacques?" Claude says. "Celebration lunch?"

"Sorry, one moment." I hold up one finger as a third message pops up on my screen, this one from Rémy.

He forwarded one he received from Maman asking if he would like to meet and that she asked me to go. As far as I am aware, this will be the first time they have spoken since we met to finalise Papa's will. Rémy sends a follow-up message.

Are you going?

I furrow my brow. It is tempting to ignore her, but something stops me. She has not made Avril's life harder, in fact after her apology and a couple of catch-ups, she went silent. I underestimated Maman.

I send a reply to Rémy first.

Yes. Are you?

Looking up at Claude then Hayden, I say, "Sorry, I cannot make it. You two go, I have somewhere to be."

Claude and Hayden share a knowing look.

"Off to Australia, hey?" Hayden asks.

He speaks the words I am already thinking. That is where I must be. If William in all his grief is reaching out, I take it as a sign Jane is not coping and she needs me.

I glance between the two men, my close friends. "Only if you two—?"

"We'll be fine," Claude and Hayden say at the same time.

"And Rémy's still around," Claude adds. "You do what you must, we'll be over the biggest hurdle soon. Just be available in case we need any signatures from you."

"Go and be with your woman," Hayden adds with a grin.

My heart skips. "Thank you. I will keep you updated."

As I stand, my phone beeps with a message from Rémy.

I will go if you go.

Chuckling, I text Maman back.

I am on my way. Meet me at Le Petit Café Parisien.

I text Rémy back with the same message and location. Finally, I send William a reply.

You do not even have to say it. I will be there as soon as I can.

Pocketing my phone, I grab my things from my office and leave in a rush. William's reply and even Maman's message have woken something in me. Last year when I was struggling, Jane flew over to support me. I tried to stop her every step of the way, even trying to end our relationship, but she did not listen and for that I am grateful. Now it is time for me to do the same for her.

It also reminded me that I still have a mother.

Jane does not.

We only ever have one biological mother in a lifetime. Papa had a lot more influence over her than I realised. It does not make any of what she did *right*, but it gives me the courage to give her one more chance. If she messes this up, I will not try again.

Time is a healer and I believe the last year softened her. And me. When Jane and I returned to the Gold Coast early last year, I wanted nothing more to do with my family. But much has changed since Papa died. *I* have changed.

I am surprised but happy that Rémy is coming to meet with Maman. It is time they talked about everything. As for Céleste, I do not know how she is feeling. She messages me and Rémy sporadically but never talks to, or about, Maman. Céleste has more baggage to wade through I suppose. Her wounds run deeper as her upbringing was so different to Rémy's and mine.

When I arrive at the café, I have received a text from Maman saying she is twenty minutes away, and one from Rémy saying he is ten minutes away.

It is a sunny and warm day today, so I sit outside and wait. People are roaming the streets going for afternoon strolls, walking pets, or eating on the run. My phone vibrates with a reply from William.

Good man. I knew I could count on you.

Grinning, I pocket my phone as Rémy arrives. He sits and grunts in greeting.

"What do you think she wants?" he asks. "To grovel?"

I shrug. "I don't know, but after Liv's death, it's made me realise I can't keep ignoring her. Life is too short to hold grudges."

Rémy nods thoughtfully. "She has explained everything to you and Céleste, yes?"

I nod and he puffs out a sigh.

"I need to hear it, but I am afraid," he confesses.

"Of?" I can still see the little boy he is inside.

He glances at the table, running his finger along the edge. "Hearing what I have always known. That I am nothing more than an unwanted child. A mistake."

"Or maybe you will hear that she knows treating you like that was wrong."

When he glances at me, there is a glimmer of hope in his eyes.

"Whatever happens though, you will have answers and closure," I add.

Maman arrives and stands beside the table, ceasing further conversation.

I do a double take and glance at Rémy who is wearing the same shocked expression. Her hair is longer, showing grey roots. Her face is not made up, and she is dressed in an out of fashion onesie. She looks old. Tired. Nothing like the all-powerful Angélique DuPont. She is a shell of her former self.

The last time I saw her like this was when Papa was in hospital.

Rémy and I stand to greet her before sitting again. At least her regal posture has not changed. Some things never will.

Maman takes her time ordering coffee, but finally does and silence comes over us while she fiddles with a napkin.

"I heard about Jane's mother," she says. "It is very upsetting news. I hope Jane is okay." There is genuine concern in her eyes.

"Are you saying it because you care, or because you have to?" I ask.

She lowers her face. "That is deserved, I suppose. I do care, it is not easy losing someone close to you."

Rémy scoffs. "You and Céleste were celebrating when Papa died."

"I am not talking about your Papa," Maman snaps. "But my children deserted me when I needed them."

"What did you expect?" Rémy blows up. "After what you and Papa put us through, and Aimée? I should not be here." He gets to his feet. "This was a mistake."

I jump up. "Rémy, cool it. Let Maman speak."

He huffs and sits again.

"I am not blind to my mistakes." Maman folds her frail looking hands on the table in front of her. "And Rémy, there is more I wish to talk to you about. Right now, I wish to apologise. For everything.

There is no one event I can choose to start from so I hope one blanket apology is enough to put us on the path of forgiveness."

Rémy scoffs again but says nothing.

"How has it gone with Aimée and Avril?" I ask instead, choosing my words carefully.

"I have not spoken to Aimée, she did not wish to see me, and I respect that. But I understand Avril fed back our meetings and conversations, and Aimée is...what is the saying? On the same page. She accepts the apology and that is enough for me. I should have handled that situation much better and I regret what happened. Avril is a lovely girl, and I am happy she got the life that she deserved."

I nod and glance at Rémy. His jaw is twitching but he does not appear to be ready to run away so that is an improvement.

"It is not easy to forgive and forget," Rémy says. "But I am willing to try. Jacques is right, losing Liv is a reminder that life is short and we only have one set of parents. Let us talk over dinner tonight."

Maman's smile of relief lights up her face, making her appear younger somehow. When she gazes at me with hope in her expression, I nod in response.

"I want to be a better mother. I will do my best. I cannot promise mistakes will not be made, but I will try."

"That is all we ask," I say, then glance at Rémy who nods.

"Now all I need is Céleste to get back to me," Maman says with a sigh. "She has not replied to me at all since we last spoke."

"She needs time," I say. "She will contact you when she is ready."

Maman sighs. "I understand." She looks from me to Rémy and adds, "About the company...Entreprises DuPont. I confess I was upset when I heard about the merger, but I realise now it is for the best. I do not need, nor do I want it on my shoulders anymore. I am very proud of how you have both handled it."

Rémy and I look at each other with wide eyes then back to Maman. "Thank you," we say in unison.

Up to this point she had never voiced her thoughts and neither of us wanted to initiate the conversation. We were cautious not to involve her in case she ever felt compelled to intervene and cause further delays. It is a relief to hear that she is no longer upset and can appreciate the benefits of our decision.

Taking in Maman and Rémy before me, hope builds in my chest. I never thought we could be a family. Too many secrets, too much pain. But meeting Jane has changed my life so much. If not for her, I would have given up on them last year. She has not only taught me patience, but that my family is not irredeemable.

She is the other half of me and that is why I must go to her. Now.

Chapter 24

Jane

M y eyes flutter open and I blink in the semi-darkness of my old bedroom. The only light coming in is through a gap in the curtains. Rolling over, I tap my phone to check the time. Ten a.m. Ugh. Can I have one more day of wallowing?

There's a gentle tap on the door.

I groan loudly into the room.

"Jane, you can't waste the day," Dad calls out.

I throw the covers back, flopping my legs on top of them. "But I want to," is what I want to say. Instead, aloud I say, "I'll be up soon."

I can't argue with him. I spent ages trying to get him up and about so it would be hypocritical of me to not push myself a bit. He turned a corner, but I've burrowed further into a black hole. I think it was a result of spending so long keeping myself and Dad afloat, the moment he started seeing the light my reserves ran dry.

"When you're ready, let's go for a walk and a coffee," he says. "We could both do with some sunshine." His footsteps fade as he disappears down the hallway.

Seconds later my door creaks open a little and Moe squeezes through. I always keep it slightly ajar so he can get in. He jumps on my bed and wastes no time sitting on my chest, looking down at me. He meows and licks my face. "Eww!" I cry with a giggle. "You've got tuna breath."

I grab him and drag him under the covers. He curls up beside me, resting his head on my arm. He starts purring and normally this lulls me back to sleep, but today I stare at the wall and let it calm me.

"What am I supposed to do, Moe?"

He stretches so his length is next to mine.

"I'm stuck." I rub his belly and he meows again. "I miss Jack." His name has Moe opening his eyes and looking at me judgingly. "Hey, don't do that. I've been lost since Mum died and I don't know how to take the first step to fix it."

He settles down again and this time falls asleep.

I think back to Jacques' message he sent a couple of days ago. I never did reply, and I feel bad. I appreciate that he's there, but taking the initiative is difficult. Now I understand what he went through last year. It's like being swallowed by darkness and escaping is next to impossible.

It doesn't help that there are too many memories at home. I love Mum, I love remembering her, but it's too much. I'm afraid Dad is struggling too, but neither of us is broaching the elephant in the room. That we don't want to stay in this house anymore.

All that aside, I miss my life. I miss Jacques. I miss Paris and the Gold Coast. I miss my job. I want the life I had before Mum died. It will never be the same without her, I'm aware of that, but it's time I learnt to adapt to the new normal. I can't bear to leave Dad on his own, but I need him to accept that staying in this house won't do him any good.

We're both stuck in a rut with no idea how to get out.

Even the wedding isn't giving me anything to look forward to. I've started receiving digital RSVP's, but it doesn't feel real. It's hard to think Mum and I did this together. Maybe this was never meant to be.

Is it time to bite the bullet and...cancel the wedding?

This thought settles like a lead weight in my stomach.

There's a knock at the front door, distracting me from my ridiculous thoughts. I'll let Dad answer it.

Tapping my phone, I check the time. Half an hour has passed. I really should get up.

The knock sounds again. Where's Dad?

"Jane!" he calls. "Can you grab that? I've got my hands in dirty water."

Ugh. I groan and sit up. It takes every ounce of energy to do so, but I succeed. Moe meows in protest but makes short work of migrating to the warmth. He curls up and instantly falls asleep.

"You're such a hog," I say. He opens one eye and I swear he's snickering.

Another knock.

"Jane!"

"I'm coming, I'm coming," I call out.

Getting to my feet, I throw on an old dressing gown and shuffle out to the hallway. Now early autumn, it's chilly this morning. We've had a cold snap that triggered the changing of the leaves. Reaching the front door, I pull it open and groan, covering my eyes with my arm. "It's so bright!"

Once my eyes adjust, I lower my arm and through the screen door, stare into familiar brown eyes and a dimpled smile.

"Jack?"

I burst into tears and fumble for the lock, flicking it across. I push the door open and throw myself at him. We embrace so tightly I can't breathe, but it's worth it.

"*Bonjour beauté*," he whispers in my ear. "I'm here. I'm always here."

As I sob into his shoulder, I feel warmth around my calves and ankles followed by meowing. Moe must've heard Jacques' voice and slipped out after me. Even if the door clicked shut, he's a smart feline and has mastered opening and pushing through doors like a pro, so long as they're not locked.

We pull away and I laugh, wiping my tears. "Moe missed you."

"Only Moe?" He reaches down to pick up the cat who settles in his arms and starts rubbing his face against Jacques'.

"I missed you too," I say, another sob rising in my throat. "I'm so sorry for—"

He leans in to silence me with a kiss, Moe rubbing his face against mine too.

"Do not be sorry for grieving," he says when he pulls away. "But we are here now, to help you and your father. We are your family too."

My heart swells with love for this man. Then it registers. "We?"

I hear an *ahem* behind me. I spin around and spot Angélique standing perfectly poised a couple of metres away, hands folded in front of her, wearing an uncertain expression.

"Angélique? Uh, hi." I glance from her to Jacques and back to her.

"Sorry to surprise you," he says, "but we were talking and"

"I believe I owe you an apology," Angélique interrupts.

She only speaks a few words but already she appears so different somehow. It's not even her longer hair, grey roots, and fashionable but understated clothes, but her whole demeanour is different. Dare I say it? She looks...*human*.

"You flew all the way out here to apologise?"

She grimaces. "Yes. I believe in making amends in person." She clears her throat delicately and lifts her head high. "Jane, I am sorry for ever making you feel inferior or uncomfortable or unwanted. I once said you would not be welcome in our family." Her voice breaks on this. A pause, then, "I would like to retract that. We have not started off on the best foot but you *are* welcome, and I hope we can get to know each other better."

My bottom lip quivers. Maybe it's because I'm over-emotional, or maybe it's because I miss Mum, but before I can stop myself I rush over and embrace her. We have never hugged. Ever. It's odd at first as she's so stiff, but she adjusts and hugs me so tight it takes me by surprise. Underneath all her thistles and thorns, she is a human. A very flawed one, but one who's trying to improve.

"I'd like that," I say.

We pull away and I'm surprised to see tears coating her cheeks. I glance back at Jacques who's smiling and scratching Moe behind the ears, who's settled on his shoulder.

The screen door creaks open and Dad steps out. "Jack, great to see you." Dad goes in for a hug, both of them slapping each other on the back. "And you must be Angélique?" he adds, turning back to us.

"Wait, you *knew*?" I ask. Dad grins and I shake my head, unable to stop the smile from stretching across my face. "Of *course* you did. You organised it, didn't you?" I sigh but go up to him and hug him. "Thanks, Dad." I step back and gesture to Angélique. "And yes, Dad, this is Jack's mother Angélique DuPont."

He steps forward, hand outstretched. "G'day, nice to meet you. I'm William Collins. Glad you could make it." He turns back to me. "Are you ready to go?"

"Oh, uh," I look from Angélique to Jacques, "we were going out for a walk and a coffee. I need to shower first, but would you both like to join us?"

They agree, and I duck back inside for a quick shower.

For the first time in weeks, there's a spark of hope. The darkness is disappearing and I can see light again. Perhaps my future with Jacques isn't doomed after all.

I'm so glad I didn't do something stupid.

➵➵➵ ⫷⫷⫷

To my surprise, Dad and Angélique get on well. *So* well in fact, I can't shut them up. There's no language barrier because Angélique's English is near perfect. I've never heard either of them talk so much before. She's not the same woman who snubbed me and told me I'd never be good enough.

So, when Jacques leans over and asks, "Can we talk?" I'm more than ready to get some fresh air. I'm sure Dad and Angélique won't mind staying at the café while they keep talking.

I nod. "You two stay here," I say to Dad and Angélique when we stand. "Jack and I are going for a walk."

They nod and start where they left off.

Some things will never cease to amaze me.

Jacques and I leave, hand in hand, to a park across the road. We stroll in silence until we arrive and enter through the gates. It's not big but it's pretty with trees, shrubs, and flowers. A path goes straight through the middle and there's a small playground, a pond with a bench on either side, and a couple of picnic settings.

We reach a bench overlooking the pond and sit. A duck waddles past and slips into the water.

"I've felt like a duck," are the first words to come out of my mouth.

Jacques chuckles and rests his arm behind me, his hand massaging my shoulder.

I glance at him and smile wryly. "You know how it appears so calm, just floats along without a care, yet under the surface its little legs are kicking like crazy."

I watch it do just that for a moment. "I've been so focused on helping Dad, on getting him back to familiar surrounds, I've been kicking and kicking in a desperate attempt to keep afloat. Over the last couple of days I couldn't kick anymore. I've put everything, including us, in jeopardy." I turn to Jacques and look him in the eye so he knows my next words are genuine. "I really am sorry. For pushing you away, for putting our relationship at—"

"Jane," he reaches out to cup my cheek, "you do not have to be sorry. I should be for not seeing sooner that you needed me." He frowns and turns away. "I suppose I have been a duck too. With the merger and everything."

I laugh but then turn to him. He leans in and presses his lips against mine, soft and promising.

"I have certainly missed your crazy talk," he says when he sits back, taking my hand in his.

"Don't worry, there's plenty more of it to come."

We sit in silence for a few moments, enjoying the closeness. Finally, I can breathe again and I think I can move on now. With that clarity comes clear thought and for the first time I realise I made another mistake.

"I don't think Dad ever wanted to come back here," I blurt, the realisation sending a shudder along my spine.

"Why do you say that?" Jacques asks.

I think back on the clues. "On our last day in Paris, he wasn't excited about going home. He did it grudgingly and probably because I gave him no choice. I never asked him what he wanted, assumed I knew best." I wince when this occurs to me. "Since we've been here, he's still struggled. He's pulled through the other side but he's not happy."

These thoughts make me realise that maybe the suggestion of selling the house won't be so difficult after all.

Hindsight is definitely a blessing *and* a curse.

"Am I a terrible daughter?" I ask, looking back at him.

He shakes his head. "Far from it. You only did what you thought was best. That makes you a great daughter. I am sure he will not hold that against you."

I nod. "Thank you, but I think Dad and I need to have a long talk." My chest swells with love for Jacques and I turn to him, squeezing his hand. "You always know the right time to turn up, don't you?"

He chuckles and shrugs. "I remember what you did for me last year and realised I needed to do the same. Sometimes we can both be too stubborn."

"I know." I huff out a sigh and laugh. "Let's try and improve that, yeah? No matter how hard it is, let's vow to always talk about what we're going through rather than doing it alone."

Jacques stands and holds out his hand. "Sounds like a plan. Now, let us keep walking."

I take his hand and he pulls me to my feet.

When we reach the other side of the park, something comes to me and I know it's the right thing. I'm not sure why, but it *feels* right.

"I think we should live in Paris. Permanently."

Jacques stops, jerking my arm in the process. I stumble back slightly and turn to him with a grin.

"But our apartment in Surfers Paradise. Your father here..." he trails off, shaking his head.

I squeeze his hand and start walking again. "We're only renting the Surfers apartment. We can either see the lease out or find someone to take it over. Either way, as much as I love it there, it makes sense that Paris is our home. With your company expanding, they need you there. And I can't deny, it's growing on me. Quite a lot actually."

He lets go of my hand and instead rests his arm over my shoulder. "And your father?"

I shrug. "I've got to give him the benefit of the doubt. He'll be okay. I'm going to suggest he sell the house when he's ready. There are too many reminders of Mum, and I think he needs the freedom to start again and just take what he wants."

He pulls me closer to him. I stumble but manage to keep in step. "You are incredible, Jane. Truly incredible. Are you sure?"

"Never been surer, but I do have one condition."

He quirks one eyebrow in question.

"I'd like a *real* home, not just an apartment. Somewhere we can settle and raise our future children."

My cheeks turn warm and I glance away. Far out, anyone would think we'd never discussed kids before. We have. A lot. But now it's so real. So close.

Jacques stops again and stares at me. There is an array of emotions in his eyes, but fear is not one of them. Over the last year, he's settled the deep-rooted fear of becoming his father. The way his eyes light up and a smile stretches across his face is proof of that.

"Then I guess we should start looking once we arrive home," he says.

"Home," I repeat. "I like the sound of that."

A ball of happiness grows in my chest and spreads through me, making me feel all warm and fuzzy inside. It's such a beautiful feeling, knowing we're both on the same page.

Grinning at each other, we continue walking, fingers linked, swinging our arms as we talk and plan our future.

Epilogue

Jane

I sit upright in bed, heart aflutter, my stomach twisting into knots.

It's here.

My wedding day. The day I marry the love of my life.

Kicking the covers aside I sit on the side of the bed, my feet resting on the wooden floorboards.

First question: do I have doubts? This is the one thing I always swore I'd ask myself when this day came. Marriage is supposed to be for a lifetime, and I'd rather not have to deal with a divorce.

I think hard for a second then laugh out loud.

Why would I have doubts after everything Jacques and I have been through?

He didn't have to follow me to Australia the first time I left Paris.

I didn't have to follow him to Paris after his father died.

Either of us could've let the relationship end after Mum died.

But we didn't because we love each other. He's my soul mate, and he's told me many times that I'm his. We are each other's futures.

Of course I don't have doubts!

Laughing, I leap out of bed and spin and dance around the room, singing badly, opening blinds and windows, anything to work off this excited energy.

It's here, it's here, it's here!

Panting from the exertion, I stop in front of the balcony doors, which I left open all night. The sheer curtains flap in the morning breeze. Stepping through, I breathe in the fresh, salty air while I take in the stunning view of white sand, turquoise water, and little accommodation huts along the shore.

The Maldives is magical. I cannot fault the service or the staff. They've been fabulous.

I only wish Mum was here.

Sighing, I rest my hands on the wooden rail and close my eyes. The balmy breeze caresses my skin and whips through my hair. If I imagine it hard enough, I can see her kissing my cheek and wishing me good luck.

Oh, how I miss her.

Dad and I have come a long way over the last few months, tumultuous though they've been. We've come out of it the other side stronger and closer than ever.

After Jacques and Angélique went back to Paris, with me promising to follow soon after, Dad surprised me with his own bombshell.

He wanted to move to Paris.

Yep, that's right. I'd already told him of our plans to make Paris home, but I hadn't expected him to want to come along. You could've knocked me down with a feather.

But I was so happy. It made it easier to suggest selling the family home. He had no hesitation and after that, everything fell into place. When I returned to Paris, Jacques and I started house hunting. Dad put his house up for sale and started the process of packing up and moving.

It took a few months, but soon enough it all came together. By the time Dad arrived, we'd settled on a house and Jacques was finalising business matters. I was there for the momentous occasion when the merger papers were signed, and I swear everyone breathed a huge sigh of relief. Until Jacques announced he wanted to expand again. Open another international office, this time in London.

Instant silence. Poor Claude looked like he was ready to keel over.

Then Jacques broke out into a grin and said he was joking. Another sigh of relief, some nervous laughter, and the two companies officially became one.

Hayden returned home a couple of days later, and he hired someone to take over my role in Australia. My workload exploded after the merger so only having to focus on Paris has made my life a lot easier.

Although if Jacques gets his way, it won't be long until we start looking at locations and staff in London. I know my soon-to-be-husband, and his expansion idea will be festering away in his mind. He knows now is not the right time. Solutions Exécutives is thriving, but it's been through a huge upheaval and the staff need time to settle. However, Jacques is determined, and an amazing businessman, he *will* succeed when the time is right.

Jacques rented out his apartment, and we moved into our spectacular Parisian home. Not only does it have a massive yard with a garden, but there is also a small cottage out the back where Dad lives. It's completely self-contained, which means he's close to us, has his own space, does his own thing, and he's only a few metres away. We're never under each other's feet. It's a great arrangement. Even Moe has settled in, although it took a while after the long flight for him to forgive me. Now he flits between our house and Dad's cottage, acting like he's king of the entire property. Typical cat.

I gasp and my eyes fly open when a knock at the door interrupts my reverie. Spinning around, I rush into the room, excitement skirting along my skin. *They're here*!

Grabbing the door handle, I pull it open so fast my hair flies back over my shoulders. I glance at the three excited faces of my bridesmaids and we all scream excitedly as we come in for a group hug while jumping up and down.

When the excitement settles down a little, Penny, Avril, and Bella go into my room chatting excitedly. They make a beeline to the closet where their dresses are, that they brought over last night. I'm about to close the door when Angélique turns a corner, a dress bag over her arm. She slows to a stop, smiling awkwardly. It was touch and go whether she'd help me get ready today, and I must admit I'm glad she's here.

She's so different nowadays. Her hair is shoulder length and she's embracing the natural grey. She looks good. Happy.

Our relationship is still a little strained, but we're both working on it. She and Jacques are on better terms but there is still tension between them. It's going to take time. Once upon a time Jacques had no intention of inviting her to the wedding, but a lot has changed. I'm glad she's here. I mean that.

"Good morning, Jane," Angélique says, all prim and proper.

I laugh and go in for a hug. She's still not much of a hugger but she'll always accept one from me. When we pull away, her cheeks are flushed and her eyes are watery, but she's smiling.

"Come in." I step back and hold the door open.

Angélique offers a tight smile and passes me into the room.

She's been emotional lately and I think it's because Céleste said she wouldn't be at the wedding. With Jacques, and even Rémy, on talking terms with her, she's eager to have Céleste on the same level but that's going to be a harder task.

Céleste's RSVP was on a postcard. Yes, that's right, *a postcard*. Sent from somewhere in the Northern Territory saying she couldn't come but wished us all the best. I was a little peeved at first, but when Jacques shrugged it off, I did too. After all, she's still on a self-discovery trip and I can't blame her for not wanting to interrupt it.

Rémy is becoming very much like his older brother. Determined, mature, and beginning to let his mother in a little more. He's been accepted into university to study medicine and will be starting in the new year. After seeing the way he was with Mum, he's going to do so well.

Old wounds are healing in the DuPont family. A family that once seemed lost forever is coming together and rebuilding. Slowly.

I close the door and turn back to see Angélique hovering near me.

"May I have one word with you?" she asks, glancing over her shoulder.

The girls are still talking and showing off their dresses, oblivious to us.

I nod and she comes closer.

In an almost whisper, she says, "I wish to...thank you for all you have done for our family." She doesn't meet my gaze. "I viewed you as a threat in the beginning, but you are far from it." She glances up and reaches out to take my hand. "You are good for my son."

I grin as she joins the girls, laying her own dress bag on the bed.

That's one hell of a compliment from Angélique, I'll take it!

When they wave me over so we can start getting ready, I join them.

⁓⟫⟫⟫ ⟪⟪⟪⁓

While Dad adjusts his tie and collar, I glance back at my bridal party waiting patiently. They're all so beautiful in their light blue dresses, hair and makeup done professionally. They've been so amazing during everything. People say you're lucky if you're blessed with one best friend in your life. I have three.

They all give me a thumbs up and I laugh.

Standing at the front is Amélie holding a basket with petals. She's twisting left and right, making the silk of her puffy skirt swish. She looks up at Penny, her eyes shining. "*Momie*! Look." And she twists again, giggling.

Penny crouches and chuckles. "Look at you, you're a princess."

Amélie grins and continues swishing.

Aimée and Tavish come rushing towards us, apologising for being late.

"You're stunning, Jane," Aimée whispers as she passes, giving my hand a quick squeeze.

They rush past and disappear down a slope to where the altar and chairs are, out of sight. I'm so happy they could make it. I remember when Jacques and I chatted to her about the wedding. How much he wanted her there, but that he understood if it would be too uncomfortable.

"I wouldn't miss it for the world," Aimée had said with tears in her eyes. "I missed out on watching you grow up. I'm not missing out on seeing you get married. I don't need to speak to Angelique and we're mature enough to not make a scene."

As far as I'm aware, Aimée and Angélique haven't spoken. I trust they won't cause problems. Yes, even Angélique. She's proven herself a lot over the past months.

The music changes from down below, indicating it's time for the girls to walk down the aisle. Their excited gasps tell me they hear it too and they need no coaxing from me. Then again, Penny will have everything under control. Considering she only had her baby four months ago, a boy named Leo, she's been the epitome of calm and confidence.

She's a lot stronger now, and with Claude still working part-time, she has all the support she needs. Claude tried once more to get Jacques to reduce the percentage of the partnership that Claude owns, but Jacques refused to change anything. Says Claude has earnt the 50/50 split. I agree wholeheartedly, and Claude has finally given up the fight.

With Henri and baby Leo in the resort's childcare for today, Penny and Claude are otherwise using this time away as a family to relax, recoup, and prepare for the new chapter of their lives.

I'm so happy for them. Who knew when this day came that we'd both be venturing down new paths in our lives?

Penny gives Amélie a gentle shove and she starts down the aisle, throwing blue and white petals along the sand. Avril steps forward, pulls her shoulders back, and after a few seconds, struts down slowly and confidently. Bella's next and as she starts the walk down, Penny sidles up to me and we embrace.

"Thank you for everything," I say. "You're the perfect matron of honour."

We pull apart and she's grinning, her cheeks tinged with pink. "And you weren't a bridezilla, so you made my life very easy. You look beautiful, Jane. I'm so happy for you."

She reaches out for my hand and squeezes then holds her bouquet in front. After a deep breath, she starts her slow walk down.

I breathe in then release it and glance at Dad through my veil. He's staring off into the distance. I loop my arm through his and give it a squeeze.

He smiles at me. "You alright, Jane?"

"Shouldn't I be asking you that?"

He gets a bit misty-eyed, but his smile doesn't falter. "Couldn't be better. I get to see my only daughter married, it's a good day."

The music changes to the bridal march and my breath catches. "Let's do this."

He pats my hand, and we begin the walk down the aisle. The altar and chairs come into view. We ended up going for small and intimate, no more than thirty guests. The merger attracted a lot of media attention so we needed a reprieve and the only journalist alerted to the location and wedding date is Jacques' trusted one. Knowing he's the only one here makes it less overwhelming.

The guests stand and Jacques turns.

He stands up straight, his brilliant, dimpled smile stretching across his face. Claude, Rémy, and Hayden are standing beside him, tall and proud in their light-coloured suits and light blue ties. Our eyes meet. Everything else disappears and my gaze remains fixed on him.

When Dad and I reach the end, he squeezes my arm before taking a front row seat. After handing my bouquet to Penny, I turn to Jacques...my soon-to-be husband. We grin at each other and any nerves I have, disappear.

"*Vous êtes si belle.*" He whispers that I'm beautiful and takes my hand.

For once in my life, I feel it. I'm *not* plain.

"*Vous êtes si beau,*" I respond in a whisper, giggling at the end when I tell him he's handsome.

He rolls his eyes playfully then we turn to the celebrant and the ceremony begins.

Overwhelming happiness bubbles up inside me and I can't stop smiling. Our life is finally beginning. We're so ready for this forever adventure.

In front of our close friends and family, with the waves lapping at the shore, and the warm, balmy, afternoon breeze caressing our skin, Jacques and I unite as one. Promising to be always together, for better or worse.

We've made three years and we're constantly learning. I'm confident we've grown stronger and while we'll always have hard times, we'll handle them better and more maturely.

"I now pronounce you husband and wife," the celebrant announces.

There's a chorus of cheers and applause as Jacques lifts my veil. His eyes are shining, full of love, as he leans in to kiss me softly, passionately, and full of promise. Every nerve ending sparks to life, my heart flutters, and I know without a single shred of doubt that this is exactly where I want my life to be.

When we pull apart, the guests still cheering and applauding, we turn back, holding hands and grin at everyone.

After we accept congratulations from everyone, they go off to do their own thing until the reception in a couple of hours. Before the photos are taken, together with Dad, Angélique, Jacques, and the wedding party, we wander down the beach a little way to a small private pier.

Reaching the end, Dad steps forward with the urn that has Mum's ashes. He takes the plastic bag out and places the urn on the wooden deck.

We'd talked about when and where to spread the ashes and could never agree. Until I suggested doing it after the ceremony and Jacques was fine with it. Not only is this our final chance to say goodbye, but we could have Mum here with us too.

Dad gestures for me to join him. I step forward with Jacques and we stand staring out over the ocean, everyone else standing behind us in respectful silence.

"I love you, Mum," I say into the breeze.

"I love you, Liv," Dad says at the same time.

He squeezes my hand then he opens the bag. After a beat of silence, he scatters the ashes onto the water, some of them catching on the breeze.

Watching the ashes disappear is freeing. I'll never *not* miss my mum, but I'm at peace now and so is Dad. Our lives can only get better from here.

Dad turns back, tears coating his cheeks, but he's smiling. To my surprise, Angélique comes over, loops her arm through his and guides him away.

"Come." Jacques takes my hand. "Let's start the next chapter of our lives."

Along with the rest of the party, we make our way down the beach to a hidden alcove for the photoshoot. Where the sand is soft and white, lined with palm trees and the sea stretches as far as the eye can see. When I saw it for myself yesterday, I knew it was perfect for the photos.

On the way there, I think about how long Jacques and I have been trying to find somewhere to call home. Somewhere to be happy. Content. Together. I always thought it was a place. A location.

But I've been handed a lot of home truths lately. The biggest one is that anywhere is home, so long as I'm with Jacques.

Also in This Series

Lonely in Paris is the first book in the series. A fun, light-hearted, billionaire romance set in the City of Love.

Jane's #1 rule in Paris: Don't fall in love

After ending a disastrous relationship, Jane accepts a job in the City of Love. The trouble is she speaks very little French, has no friends to enjoy Paris with, and she's awfully lonely.

Then she meets Jacques DuPonot.

Rich, handsome, and the cream of the Parisian crop, Jacques is living the dream. Just not his own. His father wants him to follow in his footsteps, but Jacques wants to earn his success. Trapped in a life chosen by his family, he's always been alone.

Until he meets Jane.

He's from money. She's not.
He's a planner. She's impulsive.
He's serious. She's *definitely* not.

They couldn't be more different, but they will fall. Hard.

Together Jane and Jacques will learn why Paris is the City of Love. But when an expiring visa, a jealous colleague, and manipulative family threaten their fledgling relationship, their loyalties will be tested to breaking point.

Jane broke her #1 rule, now they must decide what they are willing to sacrifice for love.

Navigate to the URL below to purchase this book.
https://books2read.com/LonelyinParis

Troubled in Paradise, the second book in this series continues Jane and Jacques' story.

Jacques' #1 goal: Start a new life in Surfers Paradise

Things are coming together nicely. A new office, new staff, and a beautiful new home.

But the news of his father's illness has Jacques troubled. Even though they cut him off a year ago, his mother and siblings beg Jacques to return to Paris and he reluctantly agrees.

When he learns a series of shocking family secrets, his world is turned upside down.

Jane is overjoyed to be back in Australia and Surfers Paradise is where they're meant to be. She has a perfect new job lined up, a renewed friendship and she's living the life.

Then Jacques returns to Paris and she receives her own earth-shattering news.

Now they need each other more than ever but they're a world apart. The pressures of distance, manipulative family and friends, and life-changing events will put their relationship to the test.

They beat the odds once before to keep their love alive. Now that trouble has reached them in paradise, they need to decide if they're willing to do it again.

Navigate to the URL below to purchase this book.

https://books2read.com/TroubledinParadise

Other Books by Lisa Stanbridge

Abandoned Hearts is my debut novel. A heartfelt story about two broken individuals who must learn to trust again.

Finally free from her abusive ex, Claire Stone accepts a job as a live-in nurse in the small beach-side town of Busselton, Western Australia. A new life is exactly what she needs. Move away, move on, forget. If only things were that simple. Even the intriguing but abrasive son of her new patient can't shield her from relentless memories.

Michael Karalis is watching his mother die while battling his ex-wife for custody of his five year old son. He's bitter, broken, and distrustful, but Claire becomes a light in his world, despite his reservations. Two broken souls need to learn to trust again and open their hearts or they'll never find the love they both need.

Navigate to the URL below to purchase this book.

https://books2read.com/AbandonedHearts

Acknowledgements

Thank you for reading **Finding Our Home**. I hope you enjoyed it.

This is the final book in the Longing for Home series. Wow! I can't get over the fact that I've released three books in 2023. Do I have regrets? No way! Am I exhausted? Hell yes! Juggling a full-time job that's insanely busy, a busy life in general, *and* releasing three books...I think it's time for a holiday.

A lot of me goes into my writing, but I found this novel especially held a lot more. I've unfortunately lost many friends, including my best friend, to cancer so when I wrote the heartbreaking scene towards the end, it came from the heart. To everyone who's experienced loss due to this horrible disease, I feel you. I really do. The pain may never go away, but you learn how to handle it better.

What's next, I hear you ask? Well, I can't formally announce it yet, but I will say it'll be a four-book series that I will release over 2024 and 2025, two books a year. I hope to release the first one in June 2024. So if you haven't already, sign up to my newsletter and you'll hear all about my upcoming releases.

As usual, there are many people to thank. People who have helped me on this journey. Not just this book or series, but my publishing journey in general.

Pete, my soul mate, husband, and proofreader. I can never thank him enough for his constant support and encouragement. I'm sure he'll be glad to have me back in the land of the living, rather than locked away in my office.

Frances Dall'Alba, my critique partner. Thank you for everything. I wouldn't be here without you.

To my beta readers, you've read every single book in this series and offered so much feedback. Thank you so much.

And last but not least, all the countless people who have offered advice or shared knowledge with me. I appreciate you all.

Thank you!

About the Author

International award-winning Australian author Lisa Stanbridge has been writing ever since she could string sentences together. As a child, it started off with princesses in castles being rescued by Prince Charming. As a teenager she moved on to angsty teens struggling through life with raging hormones. Now, as a semi-mature adult, she writes sweet contemporary romances and romantic comedies about real people going through real struggles who want their HEA.

She has been shortlisted in many contests, and even won some! Her biggest award is for her debut novel, **Abandoned Hearts**, which won 'Best First Book' in the Koru Award of Excellence, run by Romance Writers of New Zealand.

When she's not writing, Lisa works full time as a Software Tester. She reads anything she can sink her teeth into, and loves binging on

TV shows, especially the British ones. Lisa loves lazy days at the beach reading or writing, but rarely swimming, and loves spending time with her husband and her friends.

Say hello to Lisa

Visit her website and subscribe to her newsletter. It will keep you up to date with:

- New releases

- Preorder links

- New cover reveals and excerpts

And lots more!

https://lisastanbridge.wixsite.com/lisastanbridgeauthor

Leave a review

Did you enjoy this book? The best favour you can do for an author is to leave a review. If you'd like to leave one, go to your place of purchase, or search for the book on Goodreads, Amazon, or BookBub and leave a review. Thank you.